本教材受江汉大学研究生处、江汉大学外国语学院教材建设项目出版资助

英美戏剧批评教程

刘晓燕　曾　莉　主编

华中科技大学出版社
http://www.hustp.com
中国·武汉

内容提要

本书从众多有关英美戏剧的批评文章中精选数篇进行导读,以研究性思维贯穿始终,将晦涩难读的文学批评文章通过问题性指引,让学生能够基本掌握文学批评文章的研究思路与写作方法,培养学生的研究性思维,开拓其学术视野。

除用于高校英语专业研究生的课程教学外,对于英美文学爱好者,本书也是一本优秀的参考读物。

图书在版编目(CIP)数据

英美戏剧批评教程/刘晓燕,曾莉主编. —武汉:华中科技大学出版社,2021.6
ISBN 978-7-5680-7091-1

Ⅰ.①英… Ⅱ.①刘… ②曾… Ⅲ.①戏剧文学-文学评论-英国-高等学校-教材 ②戏剧文学-文学评论-美国-高等学校-教材 Ⅳ.①I561.073 ②I712.073

中国版本图书馆 CIP 数据核字(2021)第 097082 号

英美戏剧批评教程 刘晓燕 曾 莉 主编
Yingmei Xiju Piping Jiaocheng

策划编辑:刘 平
责任编辑:江旭玉
封面设计:原色设计
责任监印:周治超

出版发行:华中科技大学出版社(中国·武汉) 电话:(027)81321913
武汉市东湖新技术开发区华工科技园 邮编:430223

录 排:华中科技大学出版社美编室
印 刷:武汉开心印印刷有限公司
开 本:787mm×1092mm 1/16
印 张:11.5
字 数:218千字
版 次:2021年6月第1版第1次印刷
定 价:36.00元

本书若有印装质量问题,请向出版社营销中心调换
全国免费服务热线:400-6679-118 竭诚为您服务
版权所有 侵权必究

2020年湖北省教育厅教育科学规划项目"文化治理视野下在线课程中主体自治的方法与路径研究"（2020GB019）成果

2020年江汉大学青年教师专项教研项目"英美文学在线课程中转叙思维的应用模式与实践"（JyQ2020052）成果

Contents

Part I English Dramatists

Chapter 1   William Shakespeare .... /003

Chapter 2   George Bernard Shaw .... /033

Chapter 3   Richard Brinsley Sheridan .... /055

Chapter 4   Oscar Wilde .... /059

Chapter 5   John Osborne .... /065

Chapter 6   Samuel Beckett .... /069

Chapter 7   Harrold Pinter .... /097

Chapter 8   Tom Stoppard .... /105

Chapter 9   Caryl Churchill .... /113

Part II American Dramatists

Chapter 10   Eugene O'Neill .... /121

Chapter 11   Arthur Miller .... /133

Chapter 12   Tennessee Williams .... /141

Chapter 13　Edward Albee	/159
Chapter 14　Martha Norman	/163
Chapter 15　Susan Glaspell	/167
Chapter 16　Clifford Odets	/171

Part I English Dramatists

Chapter 1

William Shakespeare

William Shakespeare(1564-1616)

The most famous dramatist in the history of English Literature is Shakespeare. Although the language has changed since his days, each of his plays still captivates modern audiences. His dramatic works can be divided into three periods: the histories and comedies of his early period, such as *Romeo and Juliet*, *A Midsummer Night's Dream*, *The Merchant of Venice*, *The Merry Wives of Windsor*; the tragedies of the middle or "tragic" period, such as *Julius Caesar*, *Hamlet*, *Othello*, *King Lear* ; and the late period of romances or the period of serenity, such as *Winter's Tale*, and *The Tempest*. The progression of the different stages indicates his understanding of the world and humanity.

Critical Perspectives

1. Post-colonization

Ricardo Castells, in "From Caliban to Lucifer: Native Resistance and the Religious Colonization of the Indies in Baroque Spanish Theater", analyzes the drama *The Tempest* written by William Shakespeare, in the background of religious colonization and native resistance on an Mediterranean island. Topics discussed include the disastrous voyage of the Sea-Adventure which was shipwrecked off the coast of Bermuda in 1609; characters of the play including aerie spirit Ariel, the grotesque monster Caliban, and the right Duke of Milan Prospero; and illiteracy rates in Latin American nations.①

Jeevan Gurung, in "Coercion and Conversion Using Christian Magnanimity in Shakespeare's *The Tempest*", offers information on the use of Christian magnanimity in the play of William Shakespeare's *The Tempest*. Topics discussed include act of Christian magnanimity under critical scrutiny; the early history of English colonialism in the Americas; and victims of European imperialism and colonization. It also mentions dramatization of power relation in the play as the consequence of British hegemony both within and outside the country.②

Jaecheol Kim, in "The North in Shakespeare's *Richard III*", surveys William

---

① Castells R. "From Caliban to Lucifer: Native Resistance and the Religious Colonization of the Indies in Baroque Spanish Theater". Hispanófila, 2018(182):41-54.
② Gurung J. "Coercion and Conversion Using Christian Magnanimity in Shakespeare's *The Tempest*". Papers on Language & Literature, 2019, 55(4):347-367.

Shakespeare's *Richard III* in terms of the early modern construction of the north-south divide. Both modern and early modern historians view King Richard III as "England's first and only northerner king", and during his short-lived reign, the north enjoyed a time of "colonialist dominion over the South". In *Richard III*, Shakespeare engages directly with this form of colonial domination. Shakespeare's depiction of Richard III's rule projects a fear of the civilized south being colonized by the barbarous, impoverished, and militaristic north; Richard III as an "elvish-marked, abortive, rooting hog" might illustrate southern antipathy toward this northerner king. Yet Shakespeare's portrayal of him is more complicated, and *Richard III* shows how early modern England ambiguously defined the relations between the north and the south. In Shakespeare's play, Richard III is not fully northern and the north's attitude toward him is duplicitous at best. Toward the end of the narrative, Richard III is betrayed and abandoned by the northern lords, while Henry Tudor finally achieves the crown by winning over the north. In *Richard III*, Shakespeare attempts to show how much the English crown was dependent upon the north and how Tudor history was inseparably articulated with northern English history by questioning the providential rise of the Tudor dynasty. ①

Rebeca Gualberto, "Unmasking Romance in *The Tempest*: Politics, Theatre and T. S. Eliot", engages with recent postcolonial and new-historicist readings of William Shakespeare's *The Tempest* to reassess its exploitation and subversion of romance conventions, exploring an intertextual reading of Shakespeare's play and T. S. Eliot's modernist classic *The Waste Land*. The aim is to probe into the romance ideology enacted and arguably undermined in the play, going one step further from examining the interplay of the play with artistic, political and historiographical discourses and counter-discourses of the time. Taking as example

---

① Kim J. "The North in Shakespeare's *Richard III*". Studies in Philology, 2019, 116(3):451-477.

and point of reference the prominence and reinterpretation of *The Tempest* in *The Waste Land*, this article aims to explore the arguably subversive dramatization of romance in the early-modern play as belonging in a continuum of meaning that has not only inspired but actually maintains an ongoing dialogue across literary tradition.①

2. New Historicism

Dunne Derek, in "Rogues' License: Counterfeiting Authority in Early Modern Literature", demonstrates the significance of the early modern license in its myriad forms to the drama of William Shakespeare and his contemporaries. Topics discussed include analysis of originary performance of early modern drama; effort to curb the activities of rogues, vagabonds and sturdy beggars; and a play *Bartholomew Fair* by Jonson on the anxieties surrounding the early modern license.②

Patrick Gray, in "Caesar as Comic Antichrist: Shakespeare's *Julius Caesar* and the Medieval English Stage Tyran", focuses on the representation of Roman politician Julius Caesar and the Medieval English tyrant in the drama of philosopher William Shakespeare. Topics discussed include the consideration of Caesar as a comic antichrist, the vulnerability of the English drama to self-reliance, and the contrast between human vulnerability and divine power.③

Randall Martin, in "Elizabethan Civic Pageantry in *Henry VI*", examines the use of civic pageantry's characteristic style of scenic choreography in the three parts

---

① Gualberto R. "Unmasking Romance in *The Tempest*: Politics, Theatre and T. S. Eliot". Brno Studies in English, 2019, 45(1): 111-128.

② Derek D. "Rogues' License: Counterfeiting Authority in Early Modern Literature". Shakespeare Studies, 2017(45): 137-143.

③ Gray P. "Caesar as Comic Antichrist: Shakespeare's *Julius Caesar* and the Medieval English Stage Tyran". Comparative Drama, 2016, 50(1): 1-31.

of William Shakespeare's drama *Henry VI*; relationship between *Henry VI* and the aspects of Elizabethan pageantry; basic stage structures of the play; criticisms on the performance and roles of characters in the play; details of processional pageant forms incorporated in the play. [1]

S. P. Cerasano, in "'Borrowed Robes', Costume Prices, and the Drawing of *Titus Andronicus*", analyzes the drawing of the William Shakespeare drama *Titus Andronicus*, preserved among the papers of the Marquess of Bath at Longleat House, Wiltshire, Great Britain; various interpretations of the critics on the drawing; expense of clothing in the drawing; reflection of a live performance in the drawing; understanding of costuming procedures in the drawing. [2]

Stephen J. Lynch, in "Sin, Suffering, and Redemption in Leir and Lear", discusses ways in which English dramatist William Shakespeare's historical drama *King Lear* differs from the anonymous *The True Chronicle History of King Leir*; ways in which Shakespeare infused the story with a depth of spiritual concern unseen in the earlier play; depiction of a process of spiritual growth in Shakespeare's tragedy. [3]

Sidney Homan, in "Dion, Alexander, and Demetrius—Plutarch's Forgotten *Parallel Lives*—as Mirrors for Shakespeare's *Julius Caesar*", presents an essay on the observation about the neglect of comparisons between the parallel lives of Romans and Grecians in the drama *Julius Caesar*, by William Shakespeare; discussion on the trinity of Romans; explanation of the use of Plutarch by

---

[1] Martin R. "Elizabethan Civic Pageantry in *Henry VI*". University of Toronto Quarterly, 1990, 60(2):244-264.

[2] Cerasano S P. "'Borrowed Robes', Costume Prices, and the Drawing of *Titus Andronicus*". Shakespeare Studies, 1994(22):45-57.

[3] Lynch S J. "Sin, Suffering, and Redemption in Leir and Lear". Shakespeare Studies, 1986(18):161-174.

Shakespeare; indebtedness of the author to the scholarly investigation of Roman lives.①

Sara Soncini, in "Shakespeare in Sarajevo: Theatrical and Cinematic Encounters with the Balkans War", focuses on theatrical and cinematic takes that are chronologically close but geographically distant from the Yugoslav context. Katie Mitchell's staging of *Henry* VI (1994), Sarah Kane's play *Blasted* (1995) and Mario Martone's documentary-style film *Rehearsal for War* (1998) were all prompted by a deep-felt urge to confront the Bosnian war and reclaim it from the non-European otherness to which it systematically became confined in public discourse at the time. In Shakespeare, these artists found a powerful conceptual aid to universalize the conflict, as well as a means to address their discursive positioning as outsiders and its problematic implications.②

Patrick Gray, in "Shakespeare and War: Honor at the Stake", reviews scholarship to date on the question, in light of contributions to a special issue of *Critical Survey*, *Shakespeare and War*. Drawing upon St. Augustine's *The City of God*, the basis for later just war theory, Gray argues that progressive optimism regarding the perfectibility of what St. Augustine calls the City of Man makes it difficult for modern commentators to discern Shakespeare's own more tragic, Augustinian sense of warfare as a necessary evil, given the fallenness of human nature. Modern misgivings about honor also lead to misinterpretation. As Francis Fukuyama points out, present-day liberal democracies tend to follow Hobbes and Locke in attempting to "banish the desire for recognition from politics". Shakespeare in contrast, like Hegel, as well as latter-day Hegelians such as

---

① Homan S. "Dion, Alexander, and Demetrius—Plutarch's Forgotten Parallel Lives—as Mirrors for Shakespeare's *Julius Caesar*". Shakespeare Studies, 1975(8):195-210.
② Soncini S. "Shakespeare in Sarajevo: Theatrical and Cinematic Encounters with the Balkans War". Critical Survey, 2018, 30(1):26-44.

Fukuyama, Charles Taylor and Axel Honneth, sees the faculty that Plato calls thymos as an invaluable instrument of statecraft. ①

P. A. Sturrock, in "Shakespeare: The Authorship Question, a Bayesian Approach", discusses just one aspect of this major problem: whether or not the available evidence indicates that "William Shakespeare", of Stratford-upon-Avon, was a writer. We consider 24 known writers who lived in England at the same time as Shakespeare. For each of these writers, and for Shakespeare, we follow Price in considering whether or not there exists evidence in each of 10 categories relevant to the literary profession. We find that there is evidence conforming to at least 3 categories for each comparison author, but none for Shakespeare. We evaluate the probability, based on this information, that Shakespeare was a writer similar to the 24 comparison writers. According to this analysis of Price's data, we find that there is only one chance in 100,000 that Shakespeare was a writer. These considerations support the heretical view that Shakespeare was not the author of the Shakespeare material. ②

Alfred Thomas, in "Shakespeare's Bohemia: Terror and Toleration in Early Modern Europe", argues that William Shakespeare was not ignorant of the geographic location and political importance of the kingdom of Bohemia, as critics of *The Winter's Tale* have traditionally assumed since Ben Jonson's infamous jibe of 1618. Shakespeare inherited the motif of Bohemia from his source but significantly inverted it (and gave it a sea coast) in order to make Bohemia the refuge for Perdita, the outcast baby daughter of King Leontes and his wife Hermione. The paper proposes that this inversion is not coincidental but is crucial to the play's oblique message and allegorical plea for religious toleration in Jacobean England,

---

① Gray P. "Shakespeare and War: Honor at the Stake". Critical Survey, 2018, 30(1):1-25.
② Sturrock P A. "Shakespeare: The Authorship Question, a Bayesian Approach". Journal of Scientific Exploration, 2017, 31(4):677-686.

where Catholics had been persecuted since the reign of Elizabeth I. Drawing on previously overlooked primary sources by Shakespeare's Protestant and Catholic contemporaries who lived in or visited Bohemia (including Edmund Campion, John Taylor and Fynes Morison), the text demonstrates that Rudolfine Bohemia's and Prague's reputation for religious toleration in the years prior to the catastrophic *Battle of the White Mountain* (1620) would have been well-known to the playwright and his English compatriots.[①]

Kate Ravilious, in "The Bard at Home", discusses archaeological findings from the home of English playwright William Shakespeare at New Place in Stratford-upon-Avon, England. It mentions the circumstances of Shakespeare's life following the death of his son Hamnet in 1595, and his return to Stratford-upon-Avon in 1597 where he purchased the New Place house for 120 British pounds. It cites that New Place was built in 1483 as a three-story house that had more than 20 rooms, a courtyard, and two small gardens.[②]

Vladimir Brljak, in "Hamlet and the Soul-Sleepers", argues that the soliloquy, "To be, or not to be", in Shakespeare's *Hamlet* is informed by soul-sleeping: the belief that on its separation from the body at death, the soul enters an unconscious state typically described as sleep or a sleep-like stupor, in which it remains until wakened and joined with the resurrected body, and then assessed at the Last Judgment. The doctrine was advocated in some of Luther's works of the 1520s and 1530s and found acceptance among some early English Protestants, but was destined to be repudiated by later Protestant orthodoxy, and was universally condemned by mainstream Protestant thinking of Shakespeare's day. The article surveys the history of this heterodoxy in England, demonstrates its continuing

---

① Thomas A. "Shakespeare's Bohemia: Terror and Toleration in Early Modern Europe". Brno Studies in English, 2019, 45(1): 191-209.

② Ravilious K. "The Bard at Home". Archaeology, 2016, 69(4): 44-47.

significance in the late-sixteenth and early-seventeenth century, elucidates the references to the doctrine in Hamlet's soliloquy, and discusses their relevance to the broader understanding of the religious subtext of the play. ①

Kevin Ashenbach, in "'Thy Speech Serves for Authority': From Personal Fantasy to Personal Encounter in Shakespeare's *Twelfth Night*", argues that *Twelfth Night* addresses Reformation controversy by dramatizing the struggle between internal and external modes of interpretive authority as that conflict was represented in the anti-Puritan discourse of English conformist writers. ②

Evrim Doğan Adanur, in "The Uses of Anachronism in Shakespeare's *Troilus and Cressida*", argues that written at the turn of the century, *Troilus and Cressida* includes different codes of conduct in relation to those belonging to the past and the contemporary. In the play, the fading away ideals of the chivalric age are represented by the Trojan Hector and of the modern by the Greek Ulysses. William Shakespeare, by juxtaposing the medieval/feudal and the modern/capitalist in this play, employs an anachronistic approach to looking at the past and the present. In his version of the most famous story of war and valour in the Western tradition, Shakespeare problematizes the linear view of history and offers an understanding of historical difference not only by carrying contemporary forms of behavior and thought to the past but also by showing the anachronism of trying to be chivalric in the modern age. This necessary anachronism lets Shakespeare make a comment on the early modern ideology in his retelling of the seemingly Homeric tale that reached to the Renaissance in an altered form through the romance tradition. ③

---

① Brljak V. "Hamlet and the Soul-Sleepers". Reformation & Renaissance Review: Journal of the Society for Reformation Studies, 2018, 20(3):187-208.

② Ashenbach K. "'Thy Speech Serves for Authority': From Personal Fantasy to Personal Encounter in Shakespeare's *Twelfth Night*". Religion & Literature, 2018, 50(3):47-69.

③ Adanur E D. "The Uses of Anachronism in Shakespeare's *Troilus and Cressida*". Gaziantep University Journal of Social Sciences, 2017, 16(4):1048-1056.

3. Narratology

Guy Butler, in "Macbeth: 'The Great Doom's Image'", offers information on the passion story presented in the theatrical play *Macbeth* by William Shakespeare. The two types of dramas are mentioned which include Moralities and Mysteries. The use of cluster of images in order to arrive at a better understanding of certain scenes references to particular incidents in the Christian myth is cited. [1]

Margaret Litvin, in "The French Source of the Earliest Surviving Arabic *Hamlet*", explores adaptations of the drama *Hamlet* by poet William Shakespeare. The author considers an Arabic adaptation by Lebanese author Tanyus Abdu and its derivation from a text by French author Alexandre Dumas. Topics discussed include Abdu's literary career in Egypt, changes to the plot and characters, and the addition of an ending wherein the character Hamlet is triumphant instead of dead. Emphasis is given to the influence of Dumas' text on Abdus in accounting for the numerous changes made to Shakespeare's original. [2]

Joan Ozark Holmer, in "'Myself Condemned and Myself Excus'd': Tragic Effects in *Romeo and Juliet*", examines the tragic effects in William Shakespeare's drama *Romeo and Juliet*; Shakespeare's degree of success in integrating the tragic claims of fate and free will; Shakespeare's development of Romeo's statute as a tragic protagonist; effects of Shakespeare's fascination with violence on the play. [3]

---

[1] Butler G. "Macbeth: 'The Great Doom's Image'". Shakespeare in Southern Africa, 2014 (26): 75-107.

[2] Litvin M. "The French Source of the Earliest Surviving Arabic *Hamlet*". Shakespeare Studies, 2011(39): 133-151.

[3] Holmer J O. "'Myself Condemned and Myself Excus'd': Tragic Effects in *Romeo and Juliet*". Studies in Philology, 1991, 88(3): 345-362.

Jason Urbanus, in "World Roundup", presents news briefs related to archaeology. Archaeologists discovered historical artifacts in the garden of St. Louis Cathedral in New Orleans, Louisiana while excavating the area. Historical finds at an archaeological dig at Jamestown, Virginia in 2008 include a gold ring and a rare copper pendant. Archaeologists discovered the foundation of The Theatre, which hosted William Shakespeare's drama company in the 1590s. [1]

Caitlin Waits, in "A Natural Transformation: Shakespeare's Reimagining of Fairies as a Social Critique and an Observation of Ecological Anxiety", investigates the use of folklore, such as witches and fairies, in the works of playwright William Shakespeare. The topics discussed include use of folklore and legends of Shakespeare's youth, Shakespeare's employment of witches, occult, and omen in the narrative, and interpretation of the use of fairies in *A Midsummer Night's Dream*. [2]

Marjorie Garber, in "Relatable", discusses older meaning of relatable which is not only pertinent but also essential to the structure and function of many of Shakespeare's plays. It mentions playwright who is using his choric figure as a framing device for the action and elegantly crafted selfies and various settings, from home to college to sex, love, and loss. It also mentions mode of reading rather than of social action. [3]

James H. Forse, in "The Consistency of the Context: Texts and Contexts of *The Merry Wives of Windsor*", offers literary criticism of the play *The Merry Wives of Windsor* by William Shakespeare. Topics discussed include plot and character analysis of the play, Shakespeare's lack of consistency of character in his play, inconsistencies in time, place, and characters in the play, and revision of a one-

---

[1] Urbanus J. "World Roundup". Archaeology, 2019, 72(6):22-23.
[2] Waits C. "A Natural Transformation: Shakespeare's Reimagining of Fairies as a Social Critique and an Observation of Ecological Anxiety". Journal of the Wooden O, 2018(16/17):165-181.
[3] Garber M. "Relatable". Raritan, 2019, 38(4):113-129.

time Garter performance into a timelessly indeterminate comedy for the public stage.①

4. New Criticism

Geoff New, in "The Gospel according to *Romeo and Juliet*", discusses the actual meaning of Gospel in William Shakespeare's famous English Drama *Romeo and Juliet*. His drama is full of hidden gospel terms and metaphors which will attract anyone on the terms of spiritual and pious enactment. His drama has many genres such as action, suspense, comedy and romance. Its main plot is very much intensified by its sub relative plots which have caused shock, relief and despair.②

Stephen O'Neill, in "Shakespeare's Digital Flow: Humans, Technologies and the Possibilities of Intercultural Exchange", discusses that William Shakespeare is no longer fully human. He or "it", as an assemblage of texts, is now part of the information flow that characterizes the digital age. It states that Shakespeare has traditionally served as a touchstone of humanity. The word "human" is mentioned 33 times in the works themselves.③

Daniel J. Gervais, in "The Right of Attribution in Literary Works in Three Acts, by W. Shakespeare", charts the three phases in the evolution of the norm of attribution in literary works: the norm in England before and during Shakespeare's time, the emergence of authorship-based norms in the Romantic period (allowing moral rights to be enshrined in international copyright treaties) and their demise at

---

① Forse J H. "The Consistency of the Context: Texts and Contexts of *The Merry Wives of Windsor*". Journal of the Wooden O, 2018(18):18-29.

② New G. "The Gospel according to *Romeo and Juliet*". Stimulus: The New Zealand Journal of Christian Thought & Practice, 2013, 20(3):4-9.

③ O'Neill S. "Shakespeare's Digital Flow: Humans, Technologies and the Possibilities of Intercultural Exchange". Shakespeare Studies, 2018(46):120-133.

the hands of Postmodernism and New Criticism, and the current norms that aim to protect the integrity of educational processes and to inform readers and other users of books, plays, or other creative works about their "source". It tracks a debate during Shakespeare's lifetime on the difference between non-attribution and false attribution. It suggests that current attribution norms can be put in parallel with trademarks and are meant to protect both authors and the public. [1]

Darren Freebury-Jones and Marcus Dahl, in "The Limitations of Microattribution", explores methods for textual analysis of early modern plays and assesses approaches toward collecting verbal links between texts in attribution studies. As a case study, the article assesses Gary Taylor and John V. Nance's methodology—known as microattribution—for identifying word combinations within play samples that they ascribe to Marlowe. In particular, the complex verbal relations between uncontested Marlowe and Kyd texts are examined. Finally, the article proposes a new methodology for collecting collocations utilizing a shared database. [2]

Silvia Bigliazzi, in "Linguistic Taboos and the 'Unscene' of Fear in *Macbeth*", includes the presentation of fear in the play, the regicide or killing of monarchs shown in the play, and the metatheatrical transformation. It also presents views of Shakespeare on tyrants and the psychological aspects of fear. [3]

Michael Ingham and Richard Ingham, in "'Now No Way Can I Stray': Interpreting Syntactic and Semantic Role Ambiguity in Shakespeare's Dramatic Verse with Non-native Performers and Readers", discusses the study which focuses on the comprehension and production of Shakespearean language by performers and

---

[1] Gervais D J. "The Right of Attribution in Literary Works in Three Acts, by W. Shakespeare". Vanderbilt Journal of Entertainment & Technology Law, 2019, 22(1):39-70.

[2] Freebury-Jones D, Dahl M. "The Limitations of Microattribution". Texas Studies in Literature & Language, 2018, 60(4):467-495.

[3] Bigliazzi S. "Linguistic Taboos and the 'Unscene' of Fear in *Macbeth*". Comparative Drama, 2018,52(1/2):55-84.

audiences with reference to the interpretation of propositional meaning. It states that William Shakespeare's dramatic work remains of central importance to the teaching of literature worldwide, notably in the Anglophone domain wherein his work continues to be intensively studied at tertiary level. [1]

5. Canonization

Krista Rodin, in "Verdi's Faustian Otello", informs that dramas of William Shakespeare became source of inspiration for operas since enactment of *The Fairy Queen* by Henry Purcell in 1692. It is noted that the opera was based on the book *A Midsummer's Night Dream*, which late on became source of more than 200 musical theater works. It also discusses influence of composer Giuseppe Verdi on international operatic world. [2]

Scott Simmon, in "Concerning the Weary Legs of Wyatt Earp: The Classic Western according to Shakespeare", examines the incorporation of William Shakespeare's *Hamlet* in John Ford's 1946 version of the legendary Wyatt Earp in the film *My Darling Clementine*; description of the depiction of *Hamlet*; impact of the transformation of Hamlet's ethical and intellectual dilemmas; implications of recumbency in Earp's posture. [3]

Doug Stenberg, in "Tom's a-cold: Transformation and Redemption in *King Lear* and *The Fisher King*", discusses the similarities between William Shakespeare's drama *King Lear* and the motion picture *The Fisher King*, directed

---

[1] Ingham M, Ingham R. "'Now No Way Can I Stray': Interpreting Syntactic and Semantic Role Ambiguity in Shakespeare's Dramatic Verse with Non-native Performers and Readers". Shakespeare Studies, 2018(46):163-184.

[2] Rodin K. "Verdi's Faustian Otello". Interdisciplinary Humanities, 2013, 30(2):66-80.

[3] Simmon S. "Concerning the Weary Legs of Wyatt Earp: The Classic Western according to Shakespeare". Literature Film Quarterly, 1996, 24(2):114-127.

by starring Robin Williams; treatment of redemption through madness and love; importance of forgiveness; poverty, homelessness and the heroes' empathy; giving up of authority and positions in society; attempt to deny the past and return to a career; portrayal of sexual love. ①

Roy Benjamin, in "Joyce/Shakespeare: A Room of Infinite Possibilities", examines of Joyce's *Trieste Years* during which Joyce gave the *Hamlet* lectures that were the basis of the chapter, and emphasizes the importance of *Othello*, *Richard II*, *Troilus and Cressida*, and *The Tempest*. Insofar as the collection concludes with an essay on radical contextual potentiality in a Hamlet/Wake connection, the endless fertility of this old subject is affirmed and demonstrated. ②

6. Literature Geography

Kristen Poole, in "When Hell Freezes Over: Mount Hecla and Hamlet's Infernal Geography", explores the representation of purgatory in the drama *Hamlet* by author William Shakespeare in order to associate it with the Icelandic volcano of Mount Hecla. The author reflects on the relationship between supernatural geographies and cartographic sensibilities in the early modern period. Topics discussed include locating purgatory as a physical place in geography, differing theological positions on the nature of divine justice, and the inherent political dangers in representing purgatory on the Elizabethan stage during an era of Protestant reform and anti-Catholic fervor. ③

---

① Stenberg D. "Tom's a-cold: Transformation and Redemption in *King Lear* and *The Fisher King*". Literature Film Quarterly, 1994, 22(3):160-169.

② Benjamin R. "Joyce/Shakespeare: A Room of Infinite Possibilities". Journal of Modern Literature, 2018, 41(2):186-192.

③ Poole K. "When Hell Freezes Over: Mount Hecla and Hamlet's Infernal Geography". Shakespeare Studies, 2011(39):152-187.

7. Philosophical Study

Ali Shehzad Zaidi, in "Self-Contradiction in *Henry VIII* and *La cisma de Inglaterra*", examines the presence of self-contradiction in the dramas *La cisma de Inglaterra*, by Pedro Calderon de la Barca and *Henry VIII*, by William Shakespeare. The dramas are tragic in the Renaissance sense of an ambiguity that sets the limits of meaning and knowledge. Their ambiguity which lies both in their self-contradictory characters and in their historical awareness is discussed. Moreover, the article analyzes the providential Protestant and Catholic interpretations of the Reformation in the dramas.[①]

Michael McDebmott, in "A Russellian Account of Belief Sentences", discusses some brief sentences by Earl Russell, the great philosopher and writer, regarding various dramatic and historical characters. The author of the article critically apprises the one line sentences by Russell. Characters under consideration in this article are Othello and Desdimona, from the famous drama by the William Shakespeare, the greatest of all the dramatists in history of the English literature. Apart from these, the article also discusses about several other characters and belief related to Russellian account of brief sentences.[②]

Maria Valentini, in "Shakespeare's Problem Wars", investigates playwright William Shakespeare's representation and philosophy of war and peace in his works, which is called pacifism. Topics discussed include change in Shakespeare's attitude towards war in his later works, glorification of war in three parts of

---

① Zaidi A S. "Self-Contradiction in *Henry VIII* and *La cisma de Inglaterra*". Studies in Philology, 2006, 103(3):329-344.

② McDebmott M. "A Russellian Account of Belief Sentences". Philosophical Quarterly, 1988, 38(151):141-157.

Henry Ⅵ, written around 1592, and depiction of war in *King John*.①

8. Translation Study

Helena Buffery, in "Shakespeare and the Cultural Dream in Catalonia", comments on the translation made by Josep Carner on the drama *Dream* by William Shakespeare; details on the untranslatability of the imaginative world of dreams; significance on the symbolic value invested in the play; effect of complexity of rhetorical function on the translation of the poem.②

Pavel Drábek, in "Shakespeare's Myriad-Minded Stage as a Transnational Forum: Openness and Plurality in Drama Translation", discusses the essay which offers a possible reconceptualization of works derived from Shakespeare from translations through adaptations, to real-time manifestations of the Shakespeare myth. It also discusses Graham Holderness' essay which problematizes the concept of appropriation in which Holderness underpins his own approach to textual appropriations.③

Alfredo Michel Modenessi, in "'Dost Dialogue with Thy Shadow?' Translating Shakespeare Today: Tradition and Stage Business", discusses the modernity of translation which is crucial, and translating William Shakespeare's work can no longer be understood as it once was, to the point that translating them already implies working within a tradition that reaches beyond the translator's particular language and culture. It states that translating literature is best compared with

---

① Valentini M. "Shakespeare's Problem Wars". Journal of the Wooden O, 2018(16/17):138-164.

② Buffery H. "Shakespeare and the Cultural Dream in Catalonia". Journal of Iberian & Latin American Studies, 2000, 6(1):5-18.

③ Drábek P. "Shakespeare's Myriad-Minded Stage as a Transnational Forum: Openness and Plurality in Drama Translation". Shakespeare Studies, 2018(46):35-47.

playing music as to the style to which the musician subscribes and the language into which the translator works.[1]

Florence March, in "Translating Shakespeare into Postwar French Culture: The Origins of the Avignon Festival (1947)", discusses Jean Vilar who founded the Avignon Festival as a contribution to national reconstruction, a response to the urgent imperative to restore France's dignity and rebuild a sense of community following World War Ⅱ. It states that he believed in the power of arts and culture to heal, nurture and transform and Shakespeare's major influence on his implementation of a theater for all people is currently well established.[2]

9. Gender Study

Anthony Esolen, in "Hymns of the Ages", opines on the playwright William Shakespeare's drama, in which boys played most of the women's parts. Topics include music specifically written for boys to sing and written for just that instrument that produces immature male voice, and the grown man who sings that verse is conscious of the attacks not only of temptations to do wrong, but of hell itself.[3]

Charles Bell, in "'Masculine Margaret?': Margaret of Anjou's Gender Performance in Shakespeare's First", presents a discussion to understand gender roles of Margaret, one of the most popular female characters in playwright William Shakespeare's works, who appeared in tetralogy *Henry Ⅵ* Part 1, 2, and 3, and *Richard Ⅲ*. Margaret has earned admiration due to her ferocious actions that many

---

[1] Modenessi A M. "'Dost Dialogue with Thy Shadow?' Translating Shakespeare Today: Tradition and Stage Business". Shakespeare Studies, 2018(46):70-83.

[2] March F. "Translating Shakespeare into Postwar French Culture: The Origins of the Avignon Festival (1947)". Shakespeare Studies, 2018(46):59-69.

[3] Esolen A. "Hymns of the Ages". Touchstone: A Journal of Mere Christianity, 2016, 29(5):44-45.

would call her "masculine", but she also managed to retain her femininity throughout the plays by performing both the masculine and the feminine roles. [1]

Jordan Windholz, in "The Queer Testimonies of Male Chastity in *All's Well That Ends Well*", outlines the characters and explores their symbolic significance. It examines queer testimonies of male sexuality, sexual politics, marriage, and the lack of male sexual desire in the play. It also discusses the definition of male chastity. [2]

Ela Ipek Gunduz, in "Gendered Identities: Shakespeare's *The Taming of the Shrew*", argues William Shakespeare's *The Taming of the Shrew* questions the social world order that includes an exhibition of the Elizabethan norms including patriarchal authority. The subject matter of the play is a disputable topic that presents a depiction of the gender roles. The ambiguous point about Shakespeare's *The Taming of the Shrew* is the issue whether the females are surrendered to the male hegemony or not in their love relations. Throughout the centuries, both the text and the perfomance of the play are evaluated in different ways by the critics, producers and directors. Almost all interpretations add different dimensions to this controversial aspect of the play. Caroline Byrne's 2016 Globe Theatre production can be evaluated before passing onto Shakespeare's own text since it is significant to evaluate how a contemporary female director handles this problematic issue of the "taming" theme in its re-presentation of the ongoing discussions about Shakespeare's portrayal of a "tamed shrew" in the contemporary perceptions. Then, the text will be examined in its depiction of the gendered identities. [3]

---

[1] Bell C. "'Masculine Margaret?': Margaret of Anjou's Gender Performance in Shakespeare's First". Journal of the Wooden O, 2018(16/17):56-71.

[2] Windholz J. "The Queer Testimonies of Male Chastity in *All's Well That Ends Well*". Modern Philology, 2019, 116(4):322-349.

[3] Gunduz E I. "Gendered Identities: Shakespeare's *The Taming of the Shrew*". Gaziantep University Journal of Social Sciences, 2018, 17(3):834-844.

10. Reader-response Criticism

Jonas Barish, in "Is There 'Authenticity' in Theatrical Performance?", examines the presence of authenticity in the theatrical performance of William Shakespeare's plays and other English dramas which have undergone numerous revivals; attempt to re-create what the play might have looked like to its first audiences; inherent obstacles to authentic historical performance of spoken drama.①

Merlyn Q. Sell, in "How Shakespeare Lost the American West", explains playwright William Shakespeare's disappearance from the myth of the Wild West, as he was among the first European settlers in the American West, and how he has been remembered as a sign of refinement. The topics discussed include Shakespeare's large role in the Wild West of history, explanation to support why his wilder and woollier past was forgotten, and factors that played important role in his style of writing.②

Susanne Greenhalgh, in "A World Elsewhere: Documentary Representations of Social Shakespeare", focuses on the use of Shakespeare in applied theatre publicise, endorses the work of practitioners to scholars as well as the general public, and influences the growth of academic interest in what this article terms Social Shakespeare—practices in which Shakespeare and social work interact with each other to bring about change. However, in the quest for touching and uplifting individual stories, media treatments risk ignoring the actual values and strategies

---

① Barish J. "Is There 'Authenticity' in Theatrical Performance?" Modern Language Review, 1994, 89(4):817-831.
② Sell M Q. "How Shakespeare Lost the American West". Journal of the Wooden O, 2018 (16/17):28-37.

governing the work in favour of narratives that normalise social differences through emphasis on the transformative power of Shakespearean theatre. Documentaries about three different constituencies—prisoners, young people with learning disabilities, and combat veterans—are examined to determine how far they locate the need for change in society rather than in the individual. [1]

Karl Falconer, in "Getting It on Its Feet: Exploring the Politics and Process of Shakespeare outside the Traditional Classroom", examines how performance can be used as a guide for Shakespeare in education. Through this research, it aims to better question how professional theatre, community theatre and classroom education work together and learn from one another, to develop a more inclusive arts environment for those alienated by Shakespeare as a result of traditional systems. [2]

Svetlana Georgievna Kolpakova, Veronika Lubimovna Gataullina, and Ekaterina Vladimirovna Smyslova, in "Historical and Political Allusions in the Drama *Hamletmachine* by Heiner Müller", focuses on Müller's *Hamletmachine* which uses the Shakespearean plot. The authors of the article explore the new features introduced by the writer into the classic plot by placing it in postmodern principles (game, changes of meanings, rhizome, blissful ignorance of consumer society) which are woven together in a syncretic way. Müller masterfully uses these devices to transmit the political ideas and describe the history of communism and the historical events. The comparative method in combination with complex descriptive analysis of the text is chosen as the main methodology. The aim of the study is to find out what purposes and what political events Müller involves in the text of the

---

[1] Greenhalgh S. "A World Elsewhere: Documentary Representations of Social Shakespeare". Critical Survey, 2019, 31(4):77-87.

[2] Falconer K. "Getting It on Its Feet: Exploring the Politics and Process of Shakespeare outside the Traditional Classroom." Critical Survey, 2019, 31(4):42-53.

drama.①

Lauren Eriks Cline, in "Audiences Writing Race in Shakespeare Performance", explores the theatre audience's reception of race in performances of William Shakespeare's plays. Topics discussed include the role of race in the selection of actors for a particular play, the restaging of Shakespeare's plays based on cultural surroundings and preoccupations, and the critical reactions earned by the 2017 revival of Shakespeare's *The Tragedy of Julius Caesar* at the Public Theater in New York City.②

Nichole DeWall, in "Shakespeare in the Ring: Lucha Libre and *Romeo and Juliet*'s Balcony Scene", discusses the Shakespeare's ubiquity in popular culture making his plays intimidating to the modern college student. Topics include introducing students to the relationship between Shakespeare and his original audience pairing *Romeo and Juliet*'s balcony scene through digital media, and elements making students better understand the original playing conditions of the early modern playhouse especially in regards to Shakespeare's audience.③

Imran Awan, and Islam Issa, in "'Certainly the Muslim Is the Very Devil Incarnation': Islamophobia and *The Merchant of Venice*", examines Shakespeare's sixteenth-century play, *The Merchant of Venice*. Anti-Semitism is a key theme in this play. The well-known central character, Shylock, is a Jewish man ridiculed and victimised because of his identity. Much literary research has been done on the anti-Semitism of the play, and many social studies have compared anti-Semitism and Islamophobia, but scarcely any research brings a Shakespearean play from the

---

① Kolpakova S G, Gataullina V L, Smyslova E V. "Historical and Political Allusions in the Drama *Hamletmachine* by Heiner Müller". Journal of History, Culture & Art Research / Tarih Kültür ve Sanat Arastirmalari Dergisi, 2019, 8(4):313-319.

② Cline L E. "Audiences Writing Race in Shakespeare Performance". Shakespeare Studies, 2019 (47):112-119.

③ DeWall N. "Shakespeare in the Ring: Lucha Libre and *Romeo and Juliet*'s Balcony Scene". Interdisciplinary Humanities, 2019, 36(1):55-58.

sixteenth century into the context of twenty-first century Islamophobia. There are a number of similarities between the manner in which Shylock is ostracised and the current victimisation that Muslim communities are facing in Europe and more specifically the UK. With this in mind, we explore contextual and thematic elements of this play and argue that it is possible to apply the way Shylock is unfairly victimised on stage because of his identity as a Jew to the treatment of some Muslims today. In particular, the treatment he faces shares stark similarities with the types, impacts and consequences of Islamophobic hate crime today.①

Rosa Reicher, in "'Go out and Learn': Shakespeare, Bildung and the Jewish Youth Movement in Germany between Integration and Jewish Self-Identification", deals with Shakespeare's reception among German Jewish youth in the early twentieth century. The Jewish youth movements play an appreciable role in Jewish education and culture. The various Jewish youth movements reflect the German Jewish society of the time. Despite the influence of the German youth movement, the young people develop their own German Jewish Bildung canon. Many young Jews in Germany perceive Bildung as an ideal tool for full assimilation. Bildung places an emphasis on the Jewish youth as an individual, and so serves as an ideal tool for full assimilation. By means of the youth movement, German Jewish youth could develop new interpretations of identity, through the creation of a European Bildung ideal, which includes an awareness of the significance of Shakespeare.②

11. Psychoanalysis

Bernard Schweizer, in "Hamlet's 'Mousetrap' as a Wish-Fulfillment

---

① Awan I, Issa I. "'Certainly the Muslim Is the Very Devil Incarnation': Islamophobia and *The Merchant of Venice*". Muslim World, 2018, 108(3):367-386.

② Reicher R. "'Go out and Learn': Shakespeare, Bildung and the Jewish Youth Movement in Germany between Integration and Jewish Self-Identification". European Judaism, 2018, 51(2):124-133.

Dream", focuses on the psychoanalytical interpretation of the dramas *Mousetrap*, by Ernest Jones and *Hamlet*, by William Shakespeare; psychological significance of the dramas; discussion on the philosophical perspective of the dynamics of dreaming and play-acting; evaluation on the psychoanalytical indications of the dramas. [1]

Haim Omer, and Marcello Da Verona, in "Doctor Iago's Treatment of Othello", focuses on Iago's treatment of Othello in the drama *Othello* written by William Shakespeare; Iago's conversations with Othello as one of the greatest persuasive skills ever penned; full appreciation of Iago's genius; questions on how Iago thoroughly convinced and change Othello; Iago's creation of an obsession. [2]

Michael Neill, in "Shakespeare's Halle of Mirrors: Play, Politics, and Psychology in *Richard II*", focuses on the theatricality of the William Shakespeare drama *Richard III*; portrayal of the histrionic insolence of Richard; use of stage metaphors in a Marlovian pageant of self-display; example of the use of dramatic intelligence to mask limitations. [3]

Gul Kurtulus, in "A Divine Cause for Abandoning Reason in Shakespeare's *King Lear*", explores King Lear's madness in the light of new literary studies. It aims to look into the various aspects of madness that proceeds from chaos to order through the characters of King Lear and Edgar, and from blindness to healthy eyesight both in metaphoric and literal sense through the characters of King Lear and Gloucester who see better and become wiser in the end. [4]

---

[1] Schweizer B. "Hamlet's 'Mousetrap' as a Wish-Fulfillment Dream". Psychoanalytic Studies, 1999, 1(2):211-220.

[2] Omer H, Verona M D. "Doctor Iago's Treatment of Othello". American Journal of Psychotherapy, 1991, 45(1):99-112.

[3] Neill M. "Shakespeare's Halle of Mirrors: Play, Politics, and Psychology in *Richard II*". Shakespeare Studies, 1975(8):99-129.

[4] Kurtulus G. "A Divine Cause for Abandoning Reason in Shakespeare's *King Lear*". Gaziantep University Journal of Social Sciences, 2019(18):150-158.

12. Thematic Study

James L. Calderwood, in "Appalling Property in *Othello*", discusses the theme of property in the drama *Othello*, by William Shakespeare; insights on the love between characters Othello and Desdemona; depiction of Moors in the drama; views on the death of Desdemona. [1]

Beatrice Groves, in "'Now wole I a newe game begynne': Staging Suffering in *King Lear*, the Mystery Plays and Grotius's *Christus Patiens*", focuses on the link between the portrayal of violence in theatrical productions as seen in William Shakespeare's drama *King Lear* and medieval mystery plays of the same era. In *King Lear* and in most mystery plays, violence is directly enacted on the stage, whereas in classical theatrical tradition, violent scenes occur offstage. The mystery play *Christus Patiens*, by Hugo Grotius, is also discussed for its nonviolence which is not typical of its genre. [2]

Isaac Elishakoff, in "Differential Equations of Love and Love of Differential Equations", discussed against the background of William Shakespeare's *Romeo and Juliet*. In addition, a version of this relationship in a somewhat opposite setting is considered. It is proposed that engineering mathematics courses include this topic in order to promote additional interest in differential equations. In the final section, it is shown that vibration of a single-degree-of-freedom mechanical system can be cast as a love-hate relationship between its displacement and velocity, and dynamic

---

[1] Calderwood J L. "Appalling Property in *Othello*". University of Toronto Quarterly, 1988, 57 (3):353-375.

[2] Groves B. "'Now wole I a newe game begynne': Staging Suffering in *King Lear*, the Mystery Plays and Grotius's *Christus Patiens*". Medieval & Renaissance Drama in England, 2007(20):136-150.

instability identified as a transition from trigonometric love to hyperbolic. ①

Maria Valentini, in "Shakespeare's Problem Wars", investigates playwright William Shakespeare's representation and philosophy of war and peace in his works, which is called pacifism. Topics discussed include change in Shakespeare's attitude towards war in his later works, glorification of war in three parts of *Henry VI*, written around 1592, and depiction of war in *King John*. ②

John Owen Havard, in "Calculating Shylock: Commerce, Captivity, and the Free-Born Subject", focuses on eighteenth-century adaptation of William Shakespeare's play, and explores the significance of imperiled liberty depicted in *The Merchant of Venice*, enhancing and expanding upon this neglected feature of the original drama. It mentions adaptation brought this dimension of the original play together with the evolving importance of trade to England's national identity. It also mentions commercial conflict, interpersonal violence and English freedom. ③

Jeffrey R. Wilson, in "'When Evil Deeds Have Their Permissive Pass': Broken Windows in William Shakespeare's *Measure for Measure*", considers some questions of crime, criminal justice and criminology in William Shakespeare's play *Measure for Measure* (1604). In this early-modern English play, Shakespeare dramatized issues of criminology and criminal justice that Americans George Kelling and James Wilson theorized nearly four centuries later in their famous essay *Broken Windows* (1982). While this observation allows us to consider the possibility that Shakespeare was doing something like criminology centuries before there was an organized academic discipline called "criminology", a close reading of *Measure for*

---

① Elishakoff I. "Differential Equations of Love and Love of Differential Equations". Journal of Humanistic Mathematics, 2019, 9(2):226-246.

② Valentini M. "Shakespeare's Problem Wars". Journal of the Wooden O, 2018(16/17):138-164.

③ Havard J O. "Calculating Shylock: Commerce, Captivity, and the Free-Born Subject". Eighteenth Century: Theory & Interpretation (University of Pennsylvania Press), 2019, 60(3):331-350.

Measure also allows us to identify some of the faulty thinking in broken windows policing. Specifically, Shakespeare's play shows the abuses of power that can occur when individual law enforcement agents receive both a mandate to crack down on social disorder and the authority to decide for themselves what counts as disorder and how to fight it. Thus, while social scientific research and public opinion have recently called broken windows policing into question, this approach to crime control was already discredited by William Shakespeare more than 400 years ago. [1]

Evrim Doğan Adanur, in "The Trauma of Time in Shakespeare's *The Winter's Tale* and Winterson's *The Gap of Time*", evaluates the trauma of the gap of time in these two works through Cathy Caruth's theory on the effects of forgetting the past trauma and Thomas de Quincey's concept of being carried to the normal flow of time in Shakespearean dramatic action. [2]

Keith Gregor, in "Macbeth and Regimes of Reading in Francoist Spain", reports on the representation of tyrants in the William Shakespeare's play *Macbeth*. Topics mentioned include the consequences and nature of tyranny, the history of tyrants in Germany and Russia in the 20th century, and the views on tyranny shown in several books such as *The True Law of Free Monarchies* and *Basilikon Doron*. [3]

Matthew M. Davis, in "'My Master Calls Me': Authority and Loyalty in *King Lear*", focuses on the crisis of royal authority of the play *King Lear* by William Shakespeare which illustrates ways in which a king's subjects can respond to such a crisis and subjects must decide whether to preserve their loyalty to him in spite of his adversities or jettison. Those who view anthority as something defeasible are

---

[1] Wilson J R. "'When Evil Deeds Have Their Permissive Pass': Broken Windows in William Shakespeare's *Measure for Measure*". Law and Humanities, 2017,11(2):160-183.

[2] Doğan Adanur E. "The Trauma of Time in Shakespeare's *The Winter's Tale* and Winterson's *The Gap of Time*". Gaziantep University Journal of Social Science, 2018,17(2):471-478.

[3] Gregor K. "Macbeth and Regimes of Reading in Francoist Spain". Comparative Drama, 2018, 52(1/2):141-157.

prepared to accept radical revisions in terms of the status and prestige. It also mentions Shakespeare drew on political concepts of divine right. ①

13. Space Theory

Rowan Mackenzie, in "Producing Space for Shakespeare", focuses on the extent to which Shakespeare can enable those who feel imprisoned (whether literally or through social, mental, physical or economic constraints) to expand the space in which they exist. Drawing on the work of Lefebvre and Foucault in their consideration of spatial creation, manipulation and alteration by the social experiences within it, the author develops these theories to focus specifically on the use of Shakespeare's plays to evolve these, often constraining, spaces into somewhere that gives the participants the freedom and space to explore alternatives to their previous experiences of life. This article considers the impact of using Shakespeare as a method of creating space for a group of men in Leicester Prison as part of their 2017 Talent Unlocked Arts Festival. ②

14. Ethical Study

Maja Milatovic-Ovadia, in "Shakespeare's Fools: A Piece in a Peacebuilding Mosaic", analyzes the theatre project Shakespeare's Comedies performed by ethnically segregated youth in Bosnia-Herzegovina. This article aims to understand how Shakespeare's work functions as a vehicle to address the consequences of war and to support the complex process of reconciliation under circumstances in which

---

① Davis M M. "'My Master Calls Me': Authority and Loyalty in *King Lear*". Renascence, 2018, 70(1):59-78.

② Mackenzie R. "Producing Space for Shakespeare". Critical Survey, 2019, 31(4):65-76.

the issues of war crimes cannot be tackled in a straightforward and direct manner. The study takes a cross-disciplinary approach to research, drawing from theory of reconciliation, applied theatre practice and comedy studies.①

15. Eco-criticism

Katherine Steele Brokaw and Paul Prescott, in "Shakespeare in Yosemite: Applied Theatre in a National Park", describes the origins and aims of the festival within the contexts of applied theatre, eco-criticism and the American tradition of free outdoor Shakespeare. "In describing the festival's inaugural show—a collage piece that counterpointed Shakespeare's words with those of early environmentalist John Muir—we make the case for leveraging Shakespeare's cultural currency to play a part (however small or unknowable) in encouraging environmental awareness and activism."②

Caitlin Waits, in "A Natural Transformation: Shakespeare's Reimagining of Fairies as a Social Critique and an Observation of Ecological Anxiety", investigates the use of folklore, such as witches and fairies, in the works of playwright William Shakespeare. The topics discussed include use of folklore and legends of Shakespeare's youth, Shakespeare's employment of witches, occult, and omen in the narrative, and interpretation of the use of fairies in *A Midsummer Night's Dream*.③

---

① Milatovic-Ovadia M. "Shakespeare's Fools: A Piece in a Peacebuilding Mosaic". *Critical Survey*, 2019, 31(4):29-41.
② Brokaw K S, Prescott P. "Shakespeare in Yosemite: Applied Theatre in a National Park". Critical Survey, 2019, 31(4):15-28.
③ Waits C. "A Natural Transformation: Shakespeare's Reimagining of Fairies as a Social Critique and an Observation of Ecological Anxiety". Journal of the Wooden O, 2018(16/17):165-181.

16. Cultural Study

Sue Emmy Jennings, in "Thither and Back Again: An Exploration of *A Midsummer Night's Dream*", describes from the tribe in terms of understanding child attachment and development. "Finally, I suggest that Shakespeare's plays, in particular Dream, provide rites of healing. These are provided in other societies by their own culturally embedded rituals of healing."[①]

David W. Hartwig, in "The Problematic Gaze in *The Merchant of Venice*", offers literary criticism of the play *The Merchant of Venice* by William Shakespeare. Topics discussed include romantic plot and character analysis of the play, visual language that draws upon contemporary notions of visual culture in order to problematize the veracity of visual perception, and visual rhetoric in relation to the main romantic plot.[②]

Julia Reinhard Lupton, in "Patience on a Monument: Prophetic Time in Shakespeare, Fuseli, and Michelangelo", shows "how a political-theological reading of *Twelfth Night* yields a literary criticism alert to the injurious biases of inveterate prejudice and unequal power while seeking within the uneven status landscapes of Shakespearean drama and Biblical narrative signs of cosmopolitan hospitality and elastic virtue practices of attention and care".[③]

---

① Jennings S E. "Thither and Back Again: An Exploration of *A Midsummer Night's Dream*". Critical Survey, 2019, 31(4):6-14.

② Hartwig D W. "The Problematic Gaze in *The Merchant of Venice*". Journal of the Wooden O, 2018(18):30-50.

③ Lupton J R. "Patience on a Monument: Prophetic Time in Shakespeare, Fuseli, and Michelangelo". Political Theology, 2018, 19(7):653-661.

Chapter 2

George Bernard Shaw

George Bernard Shaw(1856-1950)

George Bernard Shaw's career as a dramatist began in 1892 and lasted substantially until 1939, though he wrote his last plays when he was over 80. He was a highly prolific writer. His most famous plays include *Mrs. Warren's Profession*. He is an outstanding realistic dramatist. In some of his plays, Shaw criticizes relentlessly the evils of the bourgeois society, and tears to pieces the masks of gentlemen and ladies. He won Nobel Prize in Literature in 1925.

Critical Perspectives

1. Cultural Study

Bernard McKenna, in "Yeats, *The Arrow*, and the Aesthetics of a 'National, Moral Culture': The Blanco Posnet Affair", argues that in the Irish National Theatre's little magazine, *The Arrow*, William Butler Yeats manipulates the public debate regarding George Bernard Shaw's play, *The Shewing-Up of Blanco Posnet*, to position the National Theatre at the center of nationalist movement. The result is a masterful display of political acumen that advocates the following principles: the Irish are a rational and intellectual people who possess the ability to participate in a measured and deliberate debate. They support the free expression of ideas and their authority comes from a consensus derived from discussion rather than by decree from the Crown or its representatives in the censor's office or in Dublin Castle. *The Arrow* puts forward these ideas and frames the oppositions' ideals in such a way as to place the National Theatre at the center of the debate regarding Shaw's play but also in a position of leadership within the Nationalist movement.[①]

Zafer Şafak, in "Nora's Metamorphosis in *A Doll's House* and Miss Vivie as a Paragon of the Modern Woman in *Mrs. Warren's Profession*", aims to point out and highlight the reflections of Ibsenist qualities in Shaw's *Mrs. Warren's Profession* by consolidating the clues of reverberations through *The Quintessence of Ibsenism* and by taking Ibsen's *A Doll's House* as a trajectory for proof. The study tries to prove

---

[①] McKenna B. "Yeats, *The Arrow*, and the Aesthetics of a 'National, Moral Culture': The Blanco Posnet Affair". Journal of Modern Literature, 2015,38(2):16-28.

how influential Henrik Ibsen has been in the formation of Shaw's thoughts and literary writing. In *A Doll's House*, the initial condition of submissive Nora and her ultimate transformation, and Miss Vivie, who is the unyielding and domineering protagonist of *Mrs. Warren's Profession*, are the focus of attention in the examination of how Ibsenist features surface which Shaw puts forward and favors in the "Womanly Woman" which is one of the parts of his work he titled *The Quintessence of Ibsenism*.①

2. Translation Study

Edurne Goñi Alsúa, in "Translating Characters: Eliza Doolittle 'Rendered' into Spanish", argues that *Pygmalion*, one of the best known of George Bernard Shaw's plays in Spain, was translated and performed in 1919 and published in 1920. Up to 2016, it has been rendered into Spanish five times. The main character in *Pygmalion* is Eliza, a Cockney woman who feels the need to change her life to accede to the middle class. Shaw characterized Eliza in two ways, her clothes and her speech, as she speaks the dialect of her socio-geographical background, Cockney. Translators tend to fail to do justice to Eliza's characterization for two reasons. The first is the lexical and grammatical choices, which do not always convey the same ideas as those implied in the original text. The second is the sociolinguistic disparity between the original English dialects and the Spanish dialects chosen in the translations. "We should also consider that attitudes to the social place of women have evolved in the century since *Pygmalion* was first published. In this paper, I show the different 'Elizas' which are presented in the

---

① Şafak Z. "Nora's Metamorphosis in *A Doll's House* and Miss Vivie as a Paragon of the Modern Woman in *Mrs. Warren's Profession*". Journal of Academic Studies, 2014, 16(62):125-146.

different Spanish editions of *Pygmalion*."①

3. Biographical Study

Peter Carlson, in "Gene Tunney Hits It off with George Bernard Shaw", looks at the relationship between professional boxer Gene Tunney and writer George Bernard Shaw. The author discusses Tunney's appreciation for literature and for Shaw's plays in particular, as well as Shaw's attitude towards Tunney's fighting technique. Details on a 1928 visit by Tunney and his wife Polly Lauder to Shaw's home are presented. Other topics include Shaw's book *Cashel Byron's Profession* and the depiction of the two men's relationship in the media.②

4. Narratology

Mohammad Iqbal, Amjad Ali and Ghani Rahman, in the Dilemma of Recantation and the Quest for Lamarckian Ideal in *Saint Joan*", argues that the mind-blowing confession and the subsequent recantation is a hard riddle to solve in Shaw's *Saint Joan*. The scene has already been dealt with in detail, but, to our knowledge, very little has been said about Lamarckian perspective which can brilliantly demystify the conflicting voices of the protagonist. This study highlights the dramatic worth of recantation scene and applies the literary parameters of Lamarck's theory of evolution as a tool for analyzing the conflicting attitude of *Saint Joan*. The study, however, does not recognize the scientific principles of Lamarck.

---

① Alsúa E G. "Translating Characters: Eliza Doolittle 'Rendered' into Spanish". Estudios Irlandeses, 2018, 13(2):103-119.
② Carlson P. "Gene Tunney Hits It off with George Bernard Shaw". American History, 2013, 48(5):24-25.

It takes the aesthetic and literary dimensions of the theory which the researchers have borrowed from K. M. Newton's analysis of Lamarckian and Darwinian evolution and which they have duly acknowledged in the text of the paper. ①

Craig N. Owens, in "Exorbitant Apparatus: On the Margins with Shaw, Beckett, and Joyce", examines the writings of George Bernard Shaw, an Irish dramatist. The central focus of the article is not on the plays themselves but on the texts surrounding the plays, Shaw's commentaries, prefaces, forewords and instructions of how the play in question was to be staged and interpreted. These factors are examined for a number of plays including *John Bull's Other Island*, and *Major Barbara*. It also discusses the use of supplementary texts by the Irish writers James Joyce and Samuel Beckett. ②

Bernard F. Dukore, in "Boy Gets Girl", discusses how Shaw depicts dentistry in a humorous way and comments on the romantic relationship between the characters of Gloria Clandon and Valentine in the play. The author notes that the conflict between the characters illustrates how the play follows the conventions of romantic comedies. ③

Charles A. Carpenter, in "Homo Philanderus as Created and Embodied by Bernard Shaw", compares George Bernard Shaw to the character of Leonard Charteris from Shaw's play *The Philanderer*. The author notes distinctions between dictionary definitions of the word philanderer and Shaw's conception of its meaning. Excerpts from Shaw's love letters to actresses Janet Achurch, Ellen Terry and Florence Farr are presented to demonstrate that Shaw believed philandering to be more than flirting. Shaw's attempts to woo Farr are reflected in the play by

---

① Iqbal M, Ali A, Rahman G. "The Dilemma of Recantation and the Quest for Lamarckian Ideal in Saint Joan". Putaj Humanities & Social Sciences, 2016, 23(1):11-16.

② Owens C N. "Exorbitant Apparatus: On the Margins with Shaw, Beckett, and Joyce". SHAW: The Annual of Bernard Shaw Studies, 2010,30(1):191-215.

③ Dukore B F. "Boy Gets Girl". SHAW: The Annual of Bernard Shaw Studies, 2009,29(1):28-40.

Charteris' courtship with the character of Grace Tranfield. The author comments that Charteris' rationalist views do not coincide with Shaw's views.①

5. Language Study

Andrew Cooper, in "'Worse Than Two Fathers': Steampunk *Pygmalion* and a New Look at Double Standards and the Language of Things in the Digital Realm", discusses the steampunk productions of George Bernard Shaw's play *Pygmalion*, which allows readers to see the need to reconfigure language as dynamic. Topics include embracing a destabilizing counter-pressure as a key element for future conceptualizations of language in the digital realm; the importance of understanding data governance in the digital revolution; and creating the capacity of computing language to facilitate interoperability between devices and real-time analysis of big data.②

6. Gender Study

Jennifer Janechek, in "Gendered Information Networks and the Telephone Voice in Shaw's *Pygmalion* and *Village Wooing*", considers women's contributions to the work of linguistic purification through their enforcement of the "telephone voice", a strict method of articulation taught to switchboard operators. Situating George Bernard Shaw's *Pygmalion* and *Village Wooing* in their technological climate, it argues that these plays imagine the new experience women

---

① Carpenter C A. "Homo Philanderus as Created and Embodied by Bernard Shaw". SHAW: The Annual of Bernard Shaw Studies, 2009, 29(1):4-16.

② Cooper A. "'Worse Than Two Fathers': Steampunk *Pygmalion* and a New Look at Double Standards and the Language of Things in the Digital Realm". Papers on Language and Literature, 2019, 55(4):307-346.

might have with language in a telephonic world while also searching out a mode of acoustic inscription modeled on the telephone voice that might narrow the gap between script and performance. ①

Bernard F. Dukore, in "Shaw's Way with Fanny's Untitled Play", focuses on the context of the play *Fanny's First Play*, by George Bernard Shaw which reflects on police brutality toward women. Topics discussed include the production of the play, the substitution of custom for the conscience of the play and the morality and incomprehension between parents and children of the play. ②

Philip Graham, in "Bernard Shaw's Neglected Role in English Feminism 1880-1914", argues that George Bernard Shaw has been neglected, even sometimes actively rejected by post 1970s feminist and gender historians writing about the women's emancipation movement in late Victorian and Edwardian England. This neglect is documented and contrasted with the views of feminists prior to the World War II and with those of Shaw scholars. The very significant role Shaw played in the campaigns to combat patriarchy, redefine gender roles, change the marriage laws and achieve female suffrage during this period is then described. It is shown that the arguments he uses and the language he employs have many similarities with those used by Germaine Greer. Finally, the reasons for the historical neglect of Shaw are critically considered. It is argued that, while the political views Shaw expressed in later life make his rejection understandable, far from deserving neglect he should be regarded as an inspirational influence. ③

---

① Janechek J. "Gendered Information Networks and the Telephone Voice in Shaw's *Pygmalion* and *Village Wooing*". Texas Studies in Literature & Language, 2018, 60(1):32-55.

② Dukore B F. "Shaw's Way with Fanny's Untitled Play". English Literature in Transition, 1880-1920, 2016, 59(1):25-43.

③ Graham P. "Bernard Shaw's Neglected Role in English Feminism 1880-1914". Journal of Gender Studies, 2014, 23(2):167-183.

7. New Historicism

Stanley Weintraub, in "Bernard Shaw's Unproduced Melodrama: *The Gadfly*, or *The Son of the Cardinal*", mentions that "On 23 March 1898, Bernard Shaw arranged a 'copyright performance' of a new play advertised as at the Victoria Hall in Bayswater. Typical for uncommercial exposure, the script was stapled between brown endpapers. Unlike another of his plays also 'performed' then to protect the copyright, the delicious farce *You Never Can Tell*, the melodramatic *The Gadfly* then vanished from the English stage. He had been asked by Ethel Voynich to adapt her novel for a single, minimally advertised performance to secure it from exploitation by hack dramatists always on the prowl for such prey. This article offers a discussion of all that surrounds the writing of the play, with a close exegesis of the *The Gadfly*, or *The Son of the Cardinal*."[①]

Muhammad Iqbal, and Amjad Ali, in "Shaw as an Evolutionist in *Arms and the Man*", argues that Shaw's plays are evaluated from different perspectives. Critics trace the influences of different thinkers and philosophers like Mozart, Nietzsche, Marx and Ibsen in his works. But the influences of Darwin's and Lamarck's theory of evolution have not been thoroughly and systematically discussed in his plays. There are critics like Maurice Colbourne who just casually touches upon it without making it the subject of serious discussion. This paper looks at the Shavian plays in general and *Arms and the Man* in particular within the frameworks of Darwin's and Lamarck's theories of evolution. It also aims at proving Shaw's preference for Lamarck over Darwin. The treatment of two theories of evolution would not be scientific but rather the focus would be on their literary values. The

---

① Weintraub S. "Bernard Shaw's Unproduced Melodrama: *The Gadfly*, or *The Son of the Cardinal*". English Literature in Transition, 1880-1920, 2019, 62(4):526-550.

researchers don't claim originality in deriving aesthetic and literary notions from the theories of evolution, but it is claimed with qualified assertion that the plays of Shaw in particular *Arms and the Man* bear the marks of Darwinism and Lamarckism which substantiate the originality of the study. ①

Stanley Weintraub, in "Playing the King", explores the historical and political context for George Bernard Shaw's play *The King, the Constitution and the Lady*, first published in the *Evening Standard* on December 5, 1936. Excerpts from the play are included, and parallels are drawn between it and the controversy involving Edward Ⅷ, King of England and Wallis Simpson. It is speculated that Shaw was advising Edward and the public through the newspaper that with the support of the people the King could do as he pleased. ②

James Moran, in "Meditations in Time of Civil War: *Back to Methuselah* and *Saint Joan* in Production, 1919-1924", examines aspects of the plays *Back to Methuselah*, and *Saint Joan*, works by George Bernard Shaw, an Irish dramatist. The central focus of the article is on the author's contention that Shaw was deeply involved in Irish matters throughout Ireland's war with England, during the Irish Civil War, and with the political situation in Ireland during the period from 1919 to 1924. These factors have a significant influence on *Back to Methuselah*, and *Saint Joan*, according to the author. ③

Terry Phillips, in "Shaw, Ireland, and World War Ⅰ: *O'Flaherty V. C.*, an Unlikely Recruiting Play", examines issues surrounding the World War Ⅰ and Irish independence as contained in *O'Flahery V. C.*, and to a lesser extent *Saint Joan*, plays by George Bernard Shaw, an Irish dramatist. Under discussion are the three

---

① Iqbal M, Ali A. "Shaw as an Evolutionist in *Arms and the Man*". The Dialogue, 2013, 8(2): 226-234.
② Weintraub S. "Playing the King". History Today, 2006, 56(12):20-22.
③ Moran J. "Meditations in Time of Civil War: *Back to Methuselah* and *Saint Joan* in Production, 1919-1924". SHAW: The Annual of Bernard Shaw Studies, 2010, 30(1):147-160.

issues that have an impact on Shaw's opinions on the World War Ⅰ and Ireland: the nature and impact of colonialism, socialism, and aspects of nationalism and patriotism. The article provides an overview of recruiting practices for the British armed forces conducted in Ireland. ①

Christopher Innes, in "Bernard Shaw and James B. Fagan, Playwright and Producer", examines the relationship between George Bernard Shaw and James B. Fagan, both men Irish playwrights and contemporaries. The author notes that Fagan is little remembered and many of his works relate to the early days of the motion picture industry rather to his works in the theater. Fagan's success as a theatrical producer in London, England, is examined including his productions of *Plough and the Stars*, by Sean O'Casey and plays by Luigi Pirandello and Somerset Maugham. The influence of Fagan on Shaw is discussed. ②

Nelson O'Ceallaigh Ritschel, in "Shaw and the Syngean Provocation", considers aspects of the works of dramatists George Bernard Shaw and his contemporary and fellow Irishman John Millington Synge. It is noted that Synge's first full length play *The Well of Saints*, was written in 1904 while Shaw was engaged in writing the four-act *John Bull's Other Island*. A number of issues are addressed including Shaw's and Synge's relations with William Butler Yeats, an Irish poet and dramatist, aspects related to the Irish National Theatre Society, and Irish national identity. ③

Martin Meisel, in "'Dear Harp of My Country'; Or, Shaw and Boucicault", considers aspects of the works of Irish playwrights George Bernard

---

① Phillips T. "Shaw, Ireland, and World War Ⅰ: *O'Flaherty V. C.*, an Unlikely Recruiting Play". SHAW: The Annual of Bernard Shaw Studies, 2010,30(1):133-146.

② Innes C. "Bernard Shaw and James B. Fagan, Playwright and Producer". SHAW: The Annual of Bernard Shaw Studies,2010,30(1):95-107.

③ Ritschel N O. "Shaw and the Syngean Provocation". SHAW: The Annual of Bernard Shaw Studies, 2010,30(1):75-94.

Shaw and Dion Boucicault. The author notes that Shaw was the more serious dramatist and worked on an international level, while Boucicault specialized in melodrama. According to the article, Shaw knew Boucicault's canon well, particularly the plays *The Colleen Bawn*, *The Corsican Brothers*, and *London Assurance*. The article surveys Boucicault's influence on a number of Shaw's works including *Captain Brassbound's Conversion*, *Androcles and the Lion*, and *The Devil's Disciple*. ①

Stanley Weintraub, in "Learning from Barry Sullivan: Shaw's First Superman", examines the art of acting as practiced by Barry Sullivan, an actor and theater manager in Great Britain in the 19th century. The central focus of the article is on the influence exerted by Sullivan on the plays of George Bernard Shaw, the Irish playwright. Shaw sees Sullivan on the stage in Dublin, Ireland. The author detects the influence of Sullivan in a number of Shaw's works including an early novel and in the plays *John Bull's Other Island*, *Getting Married*, and *The Apple Cart*. ②

Bernard Shaw, in "Two Unpublished Letters to Eamon de Valera", examines and discusses the text of two previously unpublished letters from George Bernard Shaw, an Irish author and playwright, to Eamon de Valera, an Irish politician. One letter, written in 1921, outlines Shaw's advice to de Valera on how he should negotiate Irish independence with the British government and with David Lloyd George, the British prime minister at the time. The second letter, written in 1946, acknowledges de Valera's expression of greetings to Shaw on the occasion of his birthday. ③

---

① Meisel M. "'Dear Harp of My Country'; Or, Shaw and Boucicault". SHAW: The Annual of Bernard Shaw Studies, 2010,30(1):43-62.

② Weintraub S. "Learning from Barry Sullivan: Shaw's First Superman". SHAW: The Annual of Bernard Shaw Studies, 2010,30(1):36-42.

③ Shaw B. "Two Unpublished Letters to Eamon de Valera". SHAW: The Annual of Bernard Shaw Studies, 2010,30(1):27-35.

Peter Gahan, in "Introduction: Bernard Shaw and the Irish Literary Tradition", discusses the Irish literary tradition and the impact that George Bernard Shaw, an Irish dramatist, has had on it. Aspects of the Irish national identity as advocated by the poet William Butler Yeats are examined, as it is the desire to escape conformity manifested by author James Joyce. The influence on several Irish literary figures, including novelist Kate O'Brien and playwright Sean O'Casey, of a number of Shaw's works are noted including *Caesar and Cleopatra*, *Man and Superman*, *John Bull's Other Island*.[1]

Reiko Oya, in "'Talk to Him': Wilde, His Friends, and Shakespeare's Sonnets", discusses the interrelationships between the author Oscar Wilde, his lover Alfred Douglas, his editor Frank Harris, and George Bernard Shaw. It notes that the drama created all of their lives by Wilde's trial for obscenity in his novel *The Picture of Dorian Gray*. It discusses the role of the sonnets of William Shakespeare in helping them all probe the depths of their feelings towards Wilde, as evidenced in letters they wrote to each other and to others.[2]

Margo Peters, in "Montgomery Davis, Bringer of Shavian Light", discusses the work of Montgomery Davis, the artistic director of the Milwaukee Chamber Theatre, in staging theatrical productions written by George Bernard Shaw. The author comments on Davis' enthusiasm for Shaw's writing due to its spiritual qualities and optimism. Davis teams with actress Ruth Schudson to stage a production of Shaw's plays *Don Juan in Hell* and *Dear Liar*, leading to the establishment of the Milwaukee Chamber Theatre. Davis' casting choices for his productions including casting actress Flora Coker in the play *Saint Joan* and actor Jonathan Smoots in the play *Man and Superman*. Economic problems faced by the

---

[1] Gahan P. "Introduction: Bernard Shaw and the Irish Literary Tradition". SHAW: The Annual of Bernard Shaw Studies, 2010, 30(1):1-26.

[2] Oya R. "'Talk to Him': Wilde, His Friends, and Shakespeare's Sonnets". Critical Survey, 2009, 21(3):22-40.

theater due to the staging of dramatic festivals are noted. ①

John H. B. Irving, in "Shaw Settles His Quarrel with Sir Henry Irving", discusses a conflict between author George Bernard Shaw and actor Henry Irving. While serving as drama critic for the periodical *Saturday Review*, Shaw makes negative comments on Irving's choice of plays following Irving's performance in the theatrical production *King Arthur*, by J. Comyns Carr. Irving's grandson Laurence Irving meets with Shaw to resolve their conflict over Shaw's comments during the pre-production of the motion picture *Pygmalion*, an adaptation of Shaw's play. Shaw's letters to Laurence Irving regarding Henry Irving's intelligence and personality are noted. Henry Irving's relationship to actress Ellen Terry is commented on. ②

Sonya Freeman Loftis, in "Shakespeare, Shotover, Surrogation: 'Blaming the Bard' in *Heartbreak House*", discusses how the work of playwright William Shakespeare influenced the writing of the theatrical production *Heartbreak House*, by George Bernard Shaw. The author suggests that Shaw intends his public persona to serve as a surrogate for Shakespeare and comments that Shaw's hostile criticism of Shakespeare conforms to scholar Joseph Roach's theory of surrogation. She suggests that *Heartbreak House* was adapted from Shakespeare's play *King Lear*, but Shaw intended to eliminate what he perceived to be aestheticism and pessimism in Shakespeare's writing. ③

Stanley Weintraub, in "Shaw's Troy: *Heartbreak House* and Euripides' *Trojan Women*", discusses how a translation by college professor Gilbert Murray of

---

① Peters M. "Montgomery Davis, Bringer of Shavian Light". SHAW: The Annual of Bernard Shaw Studies, 2009,29(1):217-225.

② Irving J H B. "Shaw Settles His Quarrel with Sir Henry Irving". SHAW: The Annual of Bernard Shaw Studies, 2009,29(1):79-91.

③ Loftis S F. "Shakespeare, Shotover, Surrogation: 'Blaming the Bard' in *Heartbreak House*". SHAW: The Annual of Bernard Shaw Studies, 2009,29(1):50-65.

the play *The Trojan Women*, by Euripides, influenced the writing of the play *Heartbreak House*, by George Bernard Shaw. The author notes that the names of characters in early drafts of *Heartbreak House* reference characters in *The Trojan Women* and that the character of Hector Hushabye in *Heartbreak House* predicts war in the same way the legendary figure of Cassandra did. He compares the character of Ariadne in *Heartbreak House* to the mythological Ariadne and notes comments by biographer Michael Holroyd suggesting that Shaw equates the fall of the British Empire to the fall of Troy in his play. The depiction of war in both plays is described.[①]

Paul Cornwell, in "Sensational with the Greeks and Daring with Shakespeare but Not So Sure about Shaw", examines theatrical productions presented at the Festival Theatre in Cambridge, England during the 1920s and 1930s. The work of theater owner and promoter Terence Gray in developing a theatre followed the model of Greek open-air theatres while incorporating modernist equipment such as directed and colored electric lighting. Particular focus is given to productions of plays written by George Bernard Shaw including *Androcles and the Lion*, produced by Herbert Prentice, *Caesar and Cleopatra*, produced by T. G. Saville, and *Heartbreak House*, produced by Cyril Wood. Gray's involvement in the Cambridge community, student involvement in the theatre, and Gray's thoughts concerning Shaw's works are explored.[②]

Stanley Weintraub, in "Disraeli in Shaw", explores the influence of statesman Benjamin Disraeli on the writing and political thinking of author George Bernard Shaw. Examples of characters resembling Disraeli appear in the plays *The Man of Destiny*, *Caesar and Cleopatra* and *Captain Brassbound's Conversion*. Other topics

---

① Weintraub S. "Shaw's Troy: *Heartbreak House* and Euripides' *Trojan Women*". SHAW: The Annual of Bernard Shaw Studies, 2009,29(1):41-49.

② Cornwell P. "Sensational with the Greeks and Daring with Shakespeare but Not So Sure about Shaw". Theatre History Studies, 2009(29):171-199.

include the rich and the poor, conservative politics, and political satire. ①

Peter Gahan, in "John Bull's Other War: Bernard Shaw and the Anglo-Irish War, 1918-1921", discusses the personal, political, and cultural commitments of Irish playwright George Bernard Shaw during the Anglo-Irish War, or Irish War of Independence, from 1918 to 1921. A year-by-year account of Shaw's activities during this period is presented, including excerpts from his letters to friends, details of his travels around the British Isles with his wife Charlotte, his views on the politics around the Irish question and the war with Great Britain, and his support for socialism and Anglo-Irish federalism. ②

Christa Zorn, in "Cosmopolitan Shaw and the Transformation of the Public Sphere", discusses the role of British writers like George Bernard Shaw and Vernon Lee as dissident public intellectuals keeping the voice of cosmopolitanism alive in Great Britain and Europe during World War I in the face of nationalism, jingoism, and government censorship. The history of the term cosmopolitan in Great Britain and Europe during the 19th and early 20th centuries is discussed, as well as the dramatic works and political writings of Shaw and Lee before, during, and after the war. ③

8. Canonization

Wendy Smith, in "The Shaw Must Go On" discusses the highlights of the Gingold Theatrical Group's Project Shaw event featuring a reading of playwright

---

① Weintraub S. "Disraeli in Shaw". English Literature in Transition, 1880-1920, 2008, 51(4): 411-420.

② Gahan P. "John Bull's Other War: Bernard Shaw and the Anglo-Irish War, 1918-1921". SHAW: The Annual of Bernard Shaw Studies, 2008, 28(1): 209-238.

③ Zorn C. "Cosmopolitan Shaw and the Transformation of the Public Sphere". SHAW: The Annual of Bernard Shaw Studies, 2008, 28(1): 188-208.

George Bernard Shaw's works. Topics covered include the Shaw New York Annual Festival launched in 2012, and the artistic director David Staller's success in enlarging the audience for Shaw in New York.①

Victor Merriman, in "Bernard Shaw in Contemporary Irish Studies: 'Passé and Contemptible'?", discusses George Bernard Shaw, an Irish dramatist, and his position in contemporary Irish Studies. Central to the article is an examination of changes in Ireland and the manner in which Irish Studies embraces or ignore those changes. Also under discussion is the role played by Shaw's play *John Bull's Other Island*, and the impact anew production of it would have on Shaw's place in the field of Irish Studies. It is noted that Irish Studies have been transformed by a number of books including *Inventing Ireland*, by Declan Kiberd, *Ireland, 1912-1985: Politics and Society*, by J. J. Lee and *Ireland and Postcolonial Theory*, by Clare Carroll and Patricia King.②

Heinz Kosok, in "John Bull's Other Eden", discusses aspects of *John Bull's Other Island*, a play by George Bernard Shaw, an Irish dramatist. The central focus of the article is the author's attempt to locate the play within the parameters of the history of Irish literature. *John Bull's Other Island* is compared to *This Other Eden*, a drama by Louis D'Alton, the action of which takes place nearly fifty years after Shaw's play. In addition, the article examines the admiration for Shaw expressed by playwright Sean O'Casey and his play *Purple Dust*.③

Brad Kent, in "Shaw, *The Bell*, and Irish Censorship in 1945", discusses George Bernard Shaw, an Irish dramatist, and the subject of censorship in Ireland. The central focus of the article is on Shaw's contribution to the debate on the

---

① Smith W. "The Shaw Must Go On". American Theatre, 2014, 31(9):54-58.
② Merriman V. "Bernard Shaw in Contemporary Irish Studies: 'Passé and Contemptible'?". SHAW: The Annual of Bernard Shaw Studies, 2010,30(1):216-235.
③ Kosok H. "John Bull's Other Eden". SHAW: The Annual of Bernard Shaw Studies, 2010,30(1):175-190.

perceived benefits of Irish censorship as conducted in the pages of *The Bell*, an Irish literary magazine. Shaw submitted an article on the subject to *The Bell* in 1945. A number of issues are addressed including Shaw's staging of plays in Ireland that were censored in England, productions of *Mrs Warren's Profession*, and informal Irish censorship of the play *John Bull's Other Island*. ①

Bernard F. Dukore, in "John MacDonald and the Washington Stage Guild", discusses the role of John MacDonald, former artistic director of the Washington Stage Guild theatrical company, in staging productions of plays written by author George Bernard Shaw. The company staged plays such as *Candida*, *The Philanderer* and *On the Rocks*. The limited budget of the company results in reduced sets and a stronger focus on actors. The author notes the popularity of the company in Washington D. C. and performances by MacDonald at the National Portrait Gallery. The relocation of the Stage Guild to different theatres and MacDonald's death due to an accident are noted. ②

Tara Stubbs, in "'Writing Was Resilience. Resilience Was an Adventure': Marianne Moore, Bernard Shaw, and the Art of Writing", discusses poetry by poet Marianne Moore regarding the influence of author George Bernard Shaw on her work. Biographer Charles Molesworth notes Moore's interest in Shaw during her education at Bryn Mawr College. Moore's poem *To a Cantankerous Poet Ignoring His Compeers—Thomas Hardy, Bernard Shaw, Joseph Conrad, Henry James* urges Shaw and other authors to tolerate each other. The author comments that Moore's poem *To Bernard Shaw: A Prize Bird* contains both praise and mockery of Shaw and addresses Shaw's alleged egotism. In her essay *Idiosyncrasy and Technique*, Moore

---

① Kent B. "Shaw, *The Bell*, and Irish Censorship in 1945". SHAW: The Annual of Bernard Shaw Studies, 2010,30(1):161-174.

② Dukore B F. "John MacDonald and the Washington Stage Guild". SHAW: The Annual of Bernard Shaw Studies, 2009,29(1):225-230.

comments on Shaw's music criticism and misquotations of his work.①

Daniel O'Leary, in "Censored and Embedded Shaw: Print Culture and Shavian Analysis of Wartime Media", discusses print culture in Great Britain around the time of World War I and its relation to the prewar and wartime writings of British playwright George Bernard Shaw, from production of his 1904 play *John Bull's Other Island* to his wartime journalism. His 1904 *Preface to Politicians* is examined for Shaw's critiques of nationalism and imperialism, as are the writings gathered in the 2006 collection *What Shaw Really Wrote About the War*, including essays such as *Common Sense About the War* (1914) and reports from the Western Front.②

9. Psychoanalysis

David Plant, in "A Look at Narcissism through Professor Higgins in *Pygmalion*", reflects upon the painful, poignant and self-inflicted inner loneliness of the narcissistic individual. In order to master early trauma, the narcissistic person constructs an outwardly substantial self in which he seeks to control others and the way he is perceived by others. In so doing he renounces the more emotionally vulnerable parts of himself, the very parts he needs in order to develop a more authentic self and emotionally connect with others. Sometimes a crack appears in his defensive narcissistic structure with the possibility of something more life-enhancing emerging.③

---

① Stubbs T. "'Writing Was Resilience. Resilience Was an Adventure': Marianne Moore, Bernard Shaw, and the Art of Writing". SHAW: The Annual of Bernard Shaw Studies, 2009,29(1):66-78.

② O'Leary D. "Censored and Embedded Shaw: Print Culture and Shavian Analysis of Wartime Media". SHAW: The Annual of Bernard Shaw Studies, 2008,28(1):168-187.

③ Plant D. "A Look at Narcissism through Professor Higgins in *Pygmalion*". British Journal of Psychotherapy, 2012, 28(1):50-65.

Nicole Coonradt, in "Shavian Romance in *Saint Joan*: Satire as Antitragedy", suggests that Shaw's play uses the presumptions of readers to redeem Joan of Arc's reputation by mixing facts and myth. She comments that the play conflicts with conventions of tragedy and attempts to reverse Joan's canonization by the Catholic Church. Shaw's depiction of Joan as lacking in physical beauty is noted. [1]

10. Comparative Study

Bert Cardullo, in "Play Doctor, Doctor Death: Shaw, Ibsen, and Modern Tragedy", examines George Bernard Shaw's *The Doctor's Dilemma* and its aspiration to tragedy. It says Shaw's critique *The Quintessence of Ibsenism* offers important pointers for analyzing the play, such as Shaw's urging that the main tragic theme in Henrik Ibsen's plays is the hopelessness of humanity's efforts to live up to the ideals it builds for itself. It says that in Shaw's play and often in Ibsen's work, these ideals on which the characters base their lives are shown to be false. [2]

Stanley Weintraub, in "Marie Corelli's Satan and *Don Juan in Hell*", presents literary criticism of *Don Juan in Hell*, an act in the play *Man and Superman*, by Irish playwright George Bernard Shaw and the book *The Sorrows of Satan* by Marie Corelli. The author discusses the literary influence of Corelli's work on the play by Shaw. The appreciation of Corelli's writing by others is also addressed, including Queen Victoria and the Prince of Wales. The characters of

---

[1] Coonradt N. "Shavian Romance in *Saint Joan*: Satire as Antitragedy". SHAW: The Annual of Bernard Shaw Studies, 2009,29(1):92-108.

[2] Cardullo B. "Play Doctor, Doctor Death: Shaw, Ibsen, and Modern Tragedy". Comparative Drama, 2011, 45(3):271-288.

Don Juan and the devil are explored.[①]

Eibhear Walshe, in "Protestant Perspectives on Ireland: *John Bull's Other Island* and *The Real Charlotte*", compares the play *John Bull's Other Island*, by George Bernard Shaw with *The Real Charlotte*, a novel about Ireland by Edith Somerville and Violet Martin and written at approximately the same time as the Shaw work. Under analysis are the social and economic conditions in Ireland at the end of the 19th century as reflected in both literary works. The central focus of the article is the author's contention that Shaw accurately predicted the future of an independent and Roman Catholic Ireland.[②]

11. Post-colonial Study

Kimberly Bohman-Kalaja, in "Undoing Identities in Two Irish Shaw Plays: *John Bull's Other Island* and *Pygmalion*", discusses aspects of the plays *John Bull's Other Island*, and *Pygmalion*, both by George Bernard Shaw, an Irish dramatist. The central focuses of the article are the identity, or lack of it, of characters in the plays, and the relation to an Irish sense of identity. The article explores the figures in each play "passing", that is, assuming characteristics they were not born with. A number of issues are examined including a post-colonial interpretation of *Pygmalion*, the reaction of poet W. B. Yeats to *John Bull's Other Island*, and Shaw and the Celtic Revival.[③]

---

① Weintraub S. "Marie Corelli's Satan and *Don Juan in Hell*". English Literature in Transition, 1880-1920, 2011, 54(2):165-173.

② Walshe E. "Protestant Perspectives on Ireland: *John Bull's Other Island* and *The Real Charlotte*". SHAW: The Annual of Bernard Shaw Studies, 2010,30(1):63-74.

③ Bohman-Kalaja K. "Undoing Identities in Two Irish Shaw Plays: *John Bull's Other Island* and *Pygmalion*". SHAW: The Annual of Bernard Shaw Studies, 2010,30(1):108-132.

12. Biographical Study

Alan Blackstock, in "'With Considerable Art' Chesterton on Blake, Browning, and Shaw", discusses the literary biographies written by G. K. Chesterton on the three artists, Robert Browning, George Bernard Shaw and William Blake. In his biographical writings, Chesterton explores the bigger issues concerning love, liberty, God and hope, and defends these subjects against the mood of pessimism and decadence. In the biographies, the artists' religious, philosophical, and intellectual influences are featured. ①

13. Postmodernism

Tony Stafford, in "Postmodern Elements in Shaw's *Misalliance*", notes the negative critical reception of the play and comments on aspects of postmodernism, such as randomness, anarchy and discontinuity, that Shaw included in this play. He suggests the characters in the play all represent Shaw's experiences and his views regarding materialism and the concept of the superman. ②

14. Musical Criticism

Peter Gahan, in "Shaw and Music: Meaning in a Basset Horn", discusses how music criticism by author George Bernard Shaw relates to baroque musical

---

① Blackstock A. "'With Considerable Art' Chesterton on Blake, Browning, and Shaw". Renascence: Essays on Values in Literature, 2009, 62(1):21-40.
② Stafford T. "Postmodern Elements in Shaw's *Misalliance*". SHAW: The Annual of Bernard Shaw Studies, 2009,29(1):176-188.

performance and Shaw's work as a playwright. The author comments on the social influence of music and the relationship of music to language. He suggests that the speaking of dialogue in Shaw's plays relates to musical performance and discusses comments made by Shaw regarding the influence of composer Wolfgang Amadeus Mozart on his writing style. [1]

---

[1] Gahan P. "Shaw and Music: Meaning in a Basset Horn". SHAW: The Annual of Bernard Shaw Studies, 2009,29(1):145-175.

Chapter 3

Richard Brinsley Sheridan

Richard Brinsley Sheridan(1751-1816)

Sheridan made great contribution to the re-survival of the play in the history of English literature: he injected fresh energy into it and helped keep it as a viable link in the continuity of the nation's dramatic tradition. Sheridan had the reputation that what ever he did was the best of its kind. His Plays, especially *The Rivials* and *The School for Scandal* were the best in his time and have since become famous world classics.

Critical Perspectives

1. Post-colonial Study

Kathleen Wilson, in "The Lure of the Other: Sheridan, Identity and Performance in Kingston and Calcutta", addresses the question through an examination of the performances of Richard Brinsley Sheridan's comic opera *The Duenna* (1775) in Kingston, Jamaica, and his comedy *The School for Scandal* (1777) in Calcutta, Bengal. In each of these sites, theatrical performances enable residents to embrace both the love of alterity and the longing for home that are each endemic to colonial life. Yet the comic figures of Jewish characters in each play suggest that Britishness and otherness are not far removed from each other, as theatrical performance, almost despite itself, begins to sketch in more similarities than differences dividing us from them. In a moment when metropolitan anxieties about empire and colonial engagements with otherness have become entangled with practices and peoples that seem to put British identity at risk, Sheridans' two comedies hint that empire could make everyone an "other", a "them". Sheridan then attempts to diffuse that insight in his plays, inviting the audience to laugh at itself as it engages in the pleasures, and pains, of real and imagined identifications.[①]

[①] Wilson K. "The Lure of the Other: Sheridan, Identity and Performance in Kingston and Calcutta". Eighteenth Century Fiction, 2015, 27(3/4):509-534.

2. New Historicism

Daniel O'Quinn, in "Navigating Crisis in Sheridan's *The Rivals*", discusses the comedy *The Rivals*, by Richard Brinsley Sheridan. The play's use of allegory, so as to suggest British policy changes towards its American colonies, is also discussed. The article references professor Lauren Berlant's perspective on fantasy to critique *The Rivals*. [1]

Barbara Roisman Cooper, in "Stage by Stage: London's Historic Theaters", focuses on various historic theaters in London, England. "Today London's well-known theaters have much the same configuration as they did back in 1663, when the Theatre Royal, Drury Lane, one of the oldest theaters in Europe, opened. Along with its neighbor, the Royal Opera House, Covent Garden, Drury Lane's history is the story of British theater from the Restoration to today." "Burned down in 1672, Drury Lane reopened in 1674; it caught fire again in 1794, when Richard Brinsley Sheridan managed it." David Garrick, who managed Drury Lane for more than two decades beginning in 1747, instituted concealed lighting. [2]

3. Biographical Study

Brooke Allen, in "The Scholar of Scandal", takes a look at Fintan O'Toole's biography of playwright, Richard Brinsley Sheridan, in his book *The Traitor's Kiss: The Life of Richard Brinsley Sheridan, 1751-1816*. The book focuses on Sheridan's

---

[1] O'Quinn D. "Navigating Crisis in Sheridan's *The Rivals*". Eighteenth Century: Theory & Interpretation (University of Pennsylvania Press), 2014, 55(1):117-122.

[2] Cooper B R. "Stage by Stage: London's Historic Theaters". British Heritage, 2006, 26(6): 34-40.

family background; education; growing up years in Bath, England; career development; highlights of his work *The Rivals*; greatest triumph as a playwright; ideas about rights and responsibilities of man.[①]

4. Psychological Study

James Thompson, in "Sheridan, *The School for Scandal*, and Aggression", discusses the manifestation of aggression in Richard Brinsley Sheridan's play *The School for Scandal*. According to the author, the play lacks a clearly privileged figure to guide the audience's response. The urbane, witty, sophisticated, and scandalous frequently manifests itself in the play in what Joseph Surface calls as the license of Invention. The author argues that the play sets up an anarchic ridicule against moralism. The play circumstantiality is privileged over abstract morality.[②]

---

① Allen B. "The Scholar of Scandal". New Criterion, 1998, 17(4):21-28.
② Thompson J. "Sheridan, *The School for Scandal*, and Aggression". Comparative Drama, 2008, 42(1):89-98.

Chapter 4

Oscar Wilde

Oscar Wilde(1854-1900)

Oscar Wilde's achievement in the field of comedy is by no means negligible. In addition to the satirical edge against the polite society of London, the plays are noted for their distinguished stylistic features. Wilde, true to form as a sensitive literary artist, managed to catch an essential part of the Victorian temper in his works.

Critical Perspectives

1. New Historicism

Wim J. C. Weren, in "Herodias and Salome in Mark's Story about the Beheading of John the Baptist", does not "provide a historical reconstruction of what exactly happened at the court of Herod Antipas, but it contains a narrative analysis of what happened in the court of Herod Antipas. This narrative analysis is followed by an intertextual approach in the second part of this article. Firstly, I will compare Mark's story with what Flavius Josephus tells about the beheading of John. Thereafter, I will highlight the roles of Herodias and Salome in the play *Salome* by Oscar Wilde from 1894, which, in turn, forms the basis of the libretto for the opera *Salome* by Richard Strauss from 1905. Do we encounter in these modern artistic recreations (Neuschöpfungen) only transformations of Mark's story, or also transgressions in which Wilde and Strauss have largely replaced the original meaning of the story with new meaning?"[①]

Eleanor Fitzsimons, in "Sarah Bernhardt, Divine Salomé", focuses on the conception of Oscar Wilde's play *Salomé*. It states that Wilde drew inspiration from the German-Jewish poet Heinrich Heine's 1843 book *Atta Troll*, in which Salomé's mother Herodias demands the severed head of John the Baptist. It also notes that Wilde's insistence on having the play performed in French in London,

---

① Weren W J C. "Herodias and Salome in Mark's Story about the Beheading of John the Baptist". Hervormde Teologiese Studies, 2019, 75(4):1-9.

England underscores its themes of isolation and language shortcomings. ①

Timothy Peltason, in "Oscar in Earnest", offers a literary criticism for the 1895 Irish play *The Importance of Being Earnest*, by Oscar Wilde. An overview of the play's depiction of power in interpersonal relations, including in regard to temporary power, empowerment, the power of transformation and the relationship between freedom and power, is provided. ②

Richard Tillinghast, in "Wilde, Synge & Orpen", comments on theater, art and culture history and developments in Dublin, Ireland. Oscar Wilde's plays continues to be played at the city including *Lady Windermere's Fan* and *The Importance of Being Earnest*. John Millington Synge's works are also staged at the Olympia theater by Galway's Druid Theater Company. Orpen's works manages to be self-conscious and referential as early as 1899, in a way that is called postmodern, while illuminating character and offering "a criticism of life". ③

2. Biographical Study

Amanda Riter, in "Villain or Victim: Transforming Salomé through Adaptation", discusses the identity, interpretations, and adaptations about Salomé, a biblical character, in plays, operas, and paintings. Topics include the play *Salomé*, by Oscar Wilde which focuses on the character's involvement in the death of religious leader John the Baptist, the book *The Antiquities of the Jews*, by Josephus which interprets the fear of Roman King Herod of John's popularity, and

---

① Fitzsimons E. "Sarah Bernhardt, Divine Salomé". History Today, 2017, 67(7):66-77.
② Peltason T. "Oscar in Earnest". Raritan, 2015, 35(1):114-144.
③ Tillinghast R. "Wilde, Synge & Orpen". The New Criterion, 2006, 24(6):31-35.

the painting titled *The Beheading of Saint John the Baptist*. ①

3. Gender Study

Im Yeeyon, in "Oscar Wilde's *Salomé*: Disorienting Orientalism", outlines the role of the characters on the issue of orientalism, spirituality, and sexuality. It examines the revelations on late Victorian constructions of gender and gay sexuality in comparison. An overview of the story of the one-act play *Salomé*, by Oscar Wilde is also given. ②

4. Canonization

Joan Navarre, in "Paul Verlaine and *A Platonic Lament*: Beardsley's Portrayal of a Parallel Love Story in Wilde's *Salomé*", presents the illustrations in *Salomé*, a play by Oscar Wilde. It explains that one of the illustrations, titled *A Platonic Lament*, is believed to contain a figure meant to be Paul Verlaine, a French poet, and the ramifications of that portrayal are discussed. The claim is made by Jean Cocteau, a French poet and filmmaker. Various interpretations of the illustration are analyzed. ③

Robert Schweik, in "Congruous Incongruities: The Wilde-Beardsley 'Collaboration'", considers an element in the relationship between Oscar Wilde's

---

① Riter A. "Villain or Victim: Transforming Salomé through Adaptation". Interdisciplinary Humanities, 2014, 31(3):18-31.

② Yeeyon I. "Oscar Wilde's *Salomé*: Disorienting Orientalism". Comparative Drama, 2011, 45(4):361-380.

③ Navarre J. "Paul Verlaine and *A Platonic Lament*: Beardsley's Portrayal of a Parallel Love Story in Wilde's *Salome*". English Literature in Transition, 1880-1920, 2008, 51(2):152-163.

play *Salomé* and Aubrey Beardsley's illustrations of the first English edition of the play, including persistence of Wilde in using matched elements in his play; incongruity in Beardsley's illustrations; analyses of Beardsley's illustrations of *Salomé*.[1]

---

[1] Schweik R. "Congruous Incongruities: The Wilde-Beardsley 'Collaboration'". English Literature in Transition, 1880-1920, 1994, 37(1):8-26.

Chapter 5

John Osborne

John Osborne (1929-1994)

John Osborne, as a preeminent English playwright, famous for his representative of the Angry Young Man that has labeled under its umbrella a number of young struggling writers of the 1950s. It has also served to categorize the group of characters in their works. His work *Look Back in Anger* was an immediate commercial success.

Critical Perspectives

1. Bibliographical Study

Jeffrey Meyers, in "Osborne's Harem", presents the women in the life of playwright John Osborne. It offers a background of the life of Osborne as a young child, as a stage actor and how he falls in love with his leading ladies. The author observes that Osborne's real life and art are symbiotic and not just simply close.[①]

2. Language Study

Philip Norman, in "What We Talk about When We Talk Nonsense", discusses the impacts of modern life on English reading and speaking. The author cites specific reference of the play *Look Back in Anger* by John Osborne, and television program *Friends*. The author also reflects on the passion of private utility company Thames Water.[②]

3. Musical Study

Alain Frogley, in "Rewriting the Renaissance: History, Imperialism, and British Music Since 1840", discusses several books concerning the history of British

---

① Meyers J. "Osborne's Harem". Antioch Review, 2009, 67(2):323-339.
② Norman P. "What We Talk about When We Talk Nonsense". New Statesman, 2015, 144/145 (5294/5295):15-16.

music since 1840: *Look Back in Anger*, by John Osborne; *Englishness: Politics and Culture, 1880-1920*, by Robert Colls and Philip Dodd; *The English Musical Renaissance, 1860-1940: Construction and Deconstruction*, by Robert Stradling and Meirion Hughes; *Imperialism and Music: Britain 1876-1953*, by Jeffrey Richards. [1]

---

[1] Frogley A. "Rewriting the Renaissance: History, Imperialism, and British Music Since 1840". Music & Letters, 2003, 84(2):241-257.

Chapter 6

Samuel Beckett

Samuel Beckett(1906-1989)

Beckett is well known as an absurd dramatist. Within his long and productive career overarching half a century from the 1930s through the post-war period, he wrote works that are strongly suggestive of the two prominent literary phases: modernism and postmodernism. He is well known for his daring formal experimentation and bringing the drama of the absurd into existence in the 1950s and 1960s. His major works include *Waiting for Godot*, *Endgame*, and *Embers*. He won the Nobel Prize in Literature in 1969.

Critical Perspectives

1. New Historicism

Megan Girdwood, in "'Danced through Its Seven Phases': Samuel Beckett, Symbolism, and Stage Choreographies", argues that allusions to dance are rife in Beckett's work, and the early development of his choreographic imagination owes much to late nineteenth-century symbolist appreciations of dance. "Symbolism's aesthetic outlook was crucially shaped by the choreographic proclivities of its key practitioners: a group that included Stéphane Mallarmé, W. B. Yeats, and Maurice Maeterlinck. In *Divagations* (1897), Mallarmé declared that both ballet and modern dance perfectly modeled the union of content and form that symbolist poetics sought to achieve. Early Beckett texts including *Dante... Bruno. Vico.. Joyce* (1929) and *Dream of Fair to Middling Women* (1932) reveal his interest in Mallarmé's theory of 'corporeal writing', while also repurposing symbolist dance forms in relation to the techniques practiced by dancers Beckett knew, including Peggy Sinclair and Lucia Joyce. These forms are condensed and developed in the late work *Quad* Ⅰ + Ⅱ (1984): an abstract play for four dancers."[①]

Camelia Anghel, in "Reading Samuel Beckett's *Endgame* as a Tale of War", focuses on the "tale of war" substratum of Samuel Beckett's 1957 play entitled *Endgame*. Containing hypothetical allusions to World War Ⅰ or Ⅱ, the drama requires a particularization of the critical perspective in the context of a Beckettian

---

① Girdwood M. "'Danced through Its Seven Phases': Samuel Beckett, Symbolism, and Stage Choreographies". Journal of Modern Literature, 2019, 42(4):74-92.

exegesis tempted to prevalently deal with generally human issues or theatre aesthetics. "Our (subjective) close reading—doubled by a (more objective) stylistic awareness—reveals that the 'war' discourse parallels (and sustains) the complementary discourse concerned with the failure of interpersonal skills, the collapse of 'plot' and 'character' or the limitations of the linguistic code."①

Lloyd (Meadhbh) Houston, in "Beckett in the Dock: Censorship, Biopolitics, and the Sinclair Trial", recovers a fuller picture of "how censorship of More Pricks affected Beckett, particularly in his attitudes to the biopolitical policing of ethnonational identity. To do so, it examines Beckett's involvement in Harry Sinclair's 1937 libel action against Oliver St. John Gogarty, and the crucial role that the suppression of More Pricks played in discrediting Beckett as a witness. In contrast to previous, 'personal' readings of the trial, it explores how the libellous passages of Gogarty's *As I Was Going Down Sackville Street* (1937) offered an anti-Semitic portrait of Sinclair and his family in which ethnic alterity and sexual deviance are presented as synonymous, and how Gogarty's barrister appropriated this rhetorical strategy to target Beckett. In the process, it offers a deep contextualisation of Beckett's anti-natalism, anti-nationalism, and longstanding aversion to censorship, by emphasising their relationship to his experiences of the operation of biopolitics in the emergent Free State and a wider European context during the trial and its aftermath."②

S. E. Gontarski, in "Ballocksed, Banjaxed or Banjoed: Textual Aberrations, Ghost Texts, and the British Godot", argues that "Censorship details of the London premiere, publication, and revival of Samuel Beckett's *Waiting for Godot* have been much discussed in the critical discourse, but that discussion has seldom been

---

① Anghel C. "Reading Samuel Beckett's *Endgame* as a Tale of War". Philologica Jassyensia, 2019, 15(1):15-24.
② Houston L (M). "Beckett in the Dock: Censorship, Biopolitics, and the Sinclair Trial". Estudios Irlandeses, 2019, 14(2):21-37.

based on the complete primary documents. As a result, erroneous and unverified information has been disseminated. In fact, the notes and correspondence in the Lord Chamberlain's archives, proscriptions demanded by the official protectors of British decency, tell a story richer and substantially different from the received wisdom on these issues. In the case of *Godot*, the tussle between Beckett and his London producer, Donald Albery, on the one hand, and on the other, three of the Lord Chamberlain's principal deputies, Sir Vincent Troubridge, Sir Norman Gwatkin, and C. D. Heriot, suggests an exchange that threatened the British production of the play. It created an atmosphere, moreover, in which English publisher Faber and Faber believed that it could offer only a sanitized version of the play in 1956."[1]

2. Reception Study

Hannah Simpson, in "Kinesthetic Empathy, Physical Recoil: The Conflicting Embodied Affects of Samuel Beckett's *Quad*", explores "audience responses to Samuel Beckett's *Quad* (1981), revealing the play's tendency to evoke intense but contradictory embodied affects for its spectator. Audience members recurrently testify to experiencing a heightened kinesthetic empathy that catalyzes their sense of identification with the onstage figures. However, they also repeatedly record a simultaneous impulse to recoil from the performers, a sense of revulsion or the refusal of immersive engagement with their moving bodies. A hybrid methodological framework of kinesthetic empathy and disability theory offers a means of better exploring both the generation and the consequence of *Quad*'s conflicting embodied affects. This framework emphasizes *Quad*'s foregrounding of its performers'

---

[1] Gontarski S E. "Ballocksed, Banjaxed or Banjoed: Textual Aberrations, Ghost Texts, and the British Godot". Journal of Modern Literature, 2018, 41(4):48-67.

embodiment, and permits a consequently clearer recognition of *Quad*'s value as a performance that demands that its spectators confront the physical fact of others' bodily existence—while acknowledging the difficulty of such engagement."①

Michelle Chiang, in "Samuel Beckett and Modernist Film Culture: Review of Samuel Beckett and Cinema", argues that "Paraskeva's monograph situates Beckett's work for the stage and screen in modernist film culture. He provides an account of Beckett's indebtedness to silent films and, more specifically, nouvelle vague film techniques. The monograph is a welcome addition to Beckett studies, and should be of interest to scholars seeking an in-depth understanding of Beckett's admiration for modernist films, and the cross-pollination of cinematic techniques in his work for stage and television."②

Alan Scott, in "A Desperate Comedy: Hope and Alienation in Samuel Beckett's *Waiting for Godot*", responses to "Samuel Beckett's *Waiting for Godot* and an examination of the concept within literature of making the strange familiar and making the familiar strange. It discusses the educative force and potential of Beckett's strangers in a strange world by examining my own personal experiences with the play. At the same time the limitations of Beckett's theatre are explored through the contrast with the work of Berthold Brecht, who sought to make the familiar strange as a method of political enquiry to facilitate the transformation of the capitalist state. Parallels are drawn between the possibilities of both theatre and education as tools for social transformation and change."③

Matthew Davies, in "'Someone Is Looking at Me Still': The Audience-

---

① Simpson H. "Kinesthetic Empathy, Physical Recoil: The Conflicting Embodied Affects of Samuel Beckett's *Quad*". Journal of Modern Literature, 2019, 42(2):132-148.

② Chiang M. "Samuel Beckett and Modernist Film Culture: Review of Samuel Beckett and Cinema". Journal of Modern Literature, 2019, 42(4):189-191.

③ Scott A. "A Desperate Comedy: Hope and Alienation in Samuel Beckett's *Waiting for Godot*". Educational Philosophy & Theory, 2013, 45(4):448-460.

Creature Relationship in the Theater Plays of Samuel Beckett", explores the nature and development of a type of audience and stage transaction in the theater plays of playwright Samuel Beckett. It examines the relationship between Beckett's creatures of illusion and the audience, which was altered over the course of his career that spanned four decades. It conceives this development in three chronological movements corresponding to the exploitation of the relationship between the auditorium and the stage by Beckett. It also explores how Beckett made metaphors of his stages, particularly in his work *Endgame*.①

Miles Beller, in "Sam I Am: The Life and Cultural Afterlife of Samuel Beckett a Century after His Birth", profiles Samuel Beckett, a Jungian analyst and a Nobel Prize winner for literary arts. Beckett's attendance on Carl Jung's lecture in London alters his thinking and writings. Several literary works of Beckett includes *Waiting for Godot*, *Watt*, and *Molloy*. Beckett's literary works continues to influence the sensibilities and consciousness of his readers even after his death in 1989.②

Judith Wechsler, in "Illustrating Samuel Beckett", suggests addressing canonical assumptions about originality and authorship with regards to artistic collaborations; illustrations for Samuel Beckett's plays; assignment of greater importance on the readings of works rather than the intentions of their producers; precedence of modernism of collaborations between writers and painters; exploration of how careers are redirected as a result of collaboration.③

---

① Davies M. "'Someone Is Looking at Me Still': The Audience-Creature Relationship in the Theater Plays of Samuel Beckett". Texas Studies in Literature & Language, 2009, 51(1):76-93.
② Beller M. "Sam I Am: The Life and Cultural Afterlife of Samuel Beckett a Century after His Birth". Psychological Perspectives, 2007, 50(2): 254-259.
③ Wechsler J. "Illustrating Samuel Beckett". Art Journal, 1993, 52(4):33-40.

3. Materiality Study

Patrick Whitmarsh, in "'So It Is I Who Speak': Communicating Bodies in Samuel Beckett's *Happy Days* and *The Unnamable*", argues that "Despite their generic and formal differences, Samuel Beckett's 1953 novel *The Unnamable* and 1961 play *Happy Days* register complementary concerns toward the relationship between embodiment and communication. Both texts exhibit aspects of what media theorists and literary critics call the materiality of communication, going so far as to imagine communication itself as re-embodiment: a process in which Beckett's compromised and sometimes indecipherable bodies discover new forms. Considering themselves as observed objects (physical and discursive), *Happy Days*'s Winnie and *The Unnamable*'s narrator reflect upon the material systems that constitute and shape them. This reflexive strategy, both aesthetic and formal, illuminates both characters' estranging physicalities at the same time that it produces them, aligning communication itself with a sense of embodiment."[1]

4. Translation Study

Lily Robert-Foley, in "*The Unnamable* de Samuel Beckett", seeks to intervene in and disrupt discourse surrounding a canonical author (Samuel Beckett), using the tools offered by reflections on (self-)translation and writing in a foreign language. These tools allow for the construction of a new, third text (in echo to Homi Bhabha's "third space"), emerging from the in-between space of Beckett's

---

[1] Whitmarsh P. "'So It Is I Who Speak': Communicating Bodies in Samuel Beckett's *Happy Days* and *The Unnamable*". Journal of Modern Literature, 2019, 42(4):111-128.

self-translations of *The Unnamable/L' Innommable*. This in-between space can be read as an invitation to bracket textual presuppositions relating to translation and to figure them in a creative way. This new, creative reading/writing of the third text springs from a well-known theme of self-translation studies to question the relationship between "original" and "translation", but specifically here in the difficulty of locating the text. This difficulty of location will be treated first in terms of time, and then space. ①

5. Aesthetic Study

Rivky Mondal, in "Malfunctioning Machines: Replaying *The Plays of Samuel Beckett* by Katherine Weiss", argues that "Samuel Beckett implemented technology at varied pressures as his plays became more abstract and austere. Progressively, machinery manifested itself less in the props and more through the effects of sound, lightning, and camera angles. In *The Plays of Samuel Beckett*, Katherine Weiss charts the constellation of technological devices in Beckett's drama. Examining Beckett's major stage, radio, and teleplays in turn, Weiss propounds that, to a large extent, machines and mechanical behavior undermine authorial ownership, perpetuate the phantasmal past, and voyeurize the audience. With no intention to systematize Beckett's theatrical practice, Weiss provides readers with durable critical tools, as she illustrates the interface of technology and technique in his dramatic oeuvre." ②

Cosmin Popovici-Toma, in "《neither》. Spectres Sonores de Samuel Beckett", argues that explicitly problematizing the relationship between music and literature,

---

① Robert-Foley L. "*The Unnamable* de Samuel Beckett". Contemporary French & Francophone Studies, 2017, 21(2):159-168.
② Mondal R. "Malfunctioning Machines: Replaying *The Plays of Samuel Beckett* by Katherine Weiss". Journal of Modern Literature, 2015, 38(2):174-177.

Chapter 6 Samuel Beckett

Samuel Beckett's *Words and Music* and *Cascando* are exemplary instances of intermediality, but only if we grasp this concept as a conceptual tool that helps us better understand the spectrality and neutrality that lie at the core of Beckett's poetics. The encounter between music and literature in these two radio plays is therefore a means of rendering paradoxically audible a ghostly absence, an aesthetic "hauntology" (Derrida) that lies neither here nor there. This unceasing hesitation nonetheless calls for a decision beyond the neuter (Blanchot): language or music; this or that? Such is the impossible task at play in *Cascando* and *Words and Music*, as well as in the rest of Beckett's works: letting the neuter be while still shaping (musical) movement. ①

Michael Kunkel, in "'... folly for t[w]o...': Samuel Beckett's *What Is the Word* and György Kurtág's *mi is a szó* Opus 30", examines "the genealogy of György Kurtág's Op. 30a and b, and their textual source, Samuel Beckett's *What Is the Word*. Beckett's attempt at a complete withdrawal from speech and at writing the absence of the subject is paralleled in Kurtág's own struggle with musical language and identity. Beckett's withdrawal behind a literary predecessor (Joyce) similarly has echoes in Kurtág's use of material from Bartók, but while Beckett's exploration of the endpoint of language is primarily an artistic exercise, Kurtág's attempts to simulate the real experience of legesthenia through the use of the (remembered) stuttering of the actress Ildikó Monyók as reciter. Op. 30b creates a larger scale piece, but maintains the stuttering formal gesture of the earlier piece, and instead of a large-scale form, uses musical palindrome to evoke the paradox of the need to speak combined with the impossibility of speech at the vanishing point of language." ②

---

① Popovici-Toma C. "《 neither 》. Spectres Sonores de Samuel Beckett". University of Toronto Quarterly, 2014, 83(3):645-658.
② Kunkel M. "'... folly for t[w]o...': Samuel Beckett's *What Is the Word* and György Kurtág's *mi is a szó* Opus 30". Contemporary Music Review, 2001, 20(2/3):109-127.

6. Linguistic Study

Ronald Schleifer, in "Modernism as Gesture: The Experience of Music, Samuel Beckett, and Performed Bewilderment", examines "gesture in music and literature—it presents a 'theory of gesture'—culminating in a close analysis of Samuel Beckett's *Not I* in the contexts of psychology and neurology. It examines gesture in relation to music, free indirect discourse in literary texts (with Joyce as example), speech-act theory, and Beckett's play as it was performed for television. In the course of its argument, it analyzes the neurobiology of gesture and signaling—from studies in cognitive psychology, evolutionary biology, and semiotics—in the context of what Colin MacCabe, following Eugene Jolas, calls 'the revolution of the word' in literary modernism. In its detailed argument, it focuses on the 'performativity' of modernist literary arts by examining literary texts—from Joyce and Beckett—in relation to gestures in music, and especially the performative gestures of popular musical performance." ①

Dilek Tüfekçi Can, in "The Representation of Anacoluthon in *Waiting for Godot* by Samuel Beckett", argues that "An absurdist play entitled *Waiting for Godot* by Samuel Beckett (1906-1989) has had received many interpretations and criticism covering a wide range of issues since its first premiere in 1953 in the Théâtre de Babylone, Paris. The play offers varying approaches for appreciating the significance of historical context in interpretation as well as the relevance of linguistic and unconscious components of the text. For instance, the play is interpreted in terms of politics, religion, psychoanalytic, homoerotic and philosophical approaches among many others. However, the play is not examined in

---

① Schleifer R. "Modernism as Gesture: The Experience of Music, Samuel Beckett, and Performed Bewilderment". Criticism, 2019, 61(1):73-96.

relation to the functions of 'anacoluthon', a linguistic term which can generally be defined as an unexpected discontinuity or disjointedness in the expression of ideas within a sentence by giving rise to a form of words in which there is logical incoherence of thought. Accordingly, in this paper firstly the demarcations between 'language' and 'culture' are exposed briefly as both of the conceptions are heavily dealt with the term 'anacoluthon'. Secondly, anacoluthon is elucidated in terms of its use and function with reference to its historical context. However, the main purpose of this paper is to unveil the functions of anacoluthon by making a classification and also to expose intra-textual functions of anacoluthon by exemplifying the discourses in order to shed light into the psychological situations of the characters and figurative meaning of the play."[1]

Elizabeth Barry, in "One's Own Company: Agency, Identity and the Middle Voice in the Work of Samuel Beckett", argues that "The concept of the middle voice, a voice denoting experience that falls between the designations of active and passive, subjective and objective, is a particularly useful one in thinking about Beckett's work. This article begins with an investigation of the linguistic concept of the middle voice and the semantic and metaphorical significance given to it in modern linguistic, psychological, and literary thought. It will then argue for its usefulness for thinking about two related aspects of Beckett's work: first, the questions of agency and the will that recur throughout Beckett's oeuvre, and second, how Beckett's early preoccupation with witness—the idea of having to be seen in order to be—transforms itself in the solitary worlds of Beckett's later works."[2]

---

[1] Tüfekçi Can D. "The Representation of Anacoluthon in *Waiting for Godot* by Samuel Beckett". Journal of Graduate School of Social Sciences, 2017, 21(1):1-17.
[2] Barry E. "One's Own Company: Agency, Identity and the Middle Voice in the Work of Samuel Beckett". Journal of Modern Literature, 2007, 31(2):115-132.

Marina Warner, in "'Who Can Shave an Egg?': Beckett, Mallarmé, and Foreign Tongues", discusses the use of foreign languages by authors, specifically Samuel Beckett and Stephane Mallarmé. Beckett uses the French language to write his work *Premier Amour*, taking advantage of special syntactical rules and connotations to add meaning and a new layer of theatricality to the book. Mallarmé, an Irishman, is a rabid student of English, and becomes so involved in the aesthetics and semantics of the language that he publishes three works on the language. The author analyzes the effects of these authors' decisions to use a foreign language when writing.①

7. Biographical Study

José Francisco Fernández, in "Surrounding the Void: Samuel Beckett and Spain", argues that "Beckett consciously abstained from having direct contact with Spanish culture and never visited Spain, despite showing an interest in the politics of the country at different periods of his life. As a result of this state of affairs a nogo area emerges which calls for a reconceptualization of Beckett's ideas on travel, politics and even his own country. This article tries to approach the matter of Beckett and Spain from different angles, in an attempt to achieve a full panoramic view. The opinions of one of Beckett's Spanish friends, Manolo Fandos, are recorded here for the first time."②

---

① Warner M. "'Who Can Shave an Egg?': Beckett, Mallarmé, and Foreign Tongues". Raritan, 2008, 27(4):62-89.
② Francisco Fernández J. "Surrounding the Void: Samuel Beckett and Spain". Estudios Irlandeses, 2014(9):44-53.

8. Philosophical Study

Iulia Luca, in "The Nothingness in Samuel Beckett's Prose Writing *How It Is* as an Aesthetic Concept", argues that Samuel Beckett presents the futility and illogicality of the human condition. He does not present single destinies but tends to generalize the destiny of the individual. With him the totality of the human condition is the one that comes to be questioned, not the man of a certain society, not even the man alienated by a certain ideology which simplifies and modifies at the same time the historic and metaphysical reality, the authentic reality into which man is integrated. Therefore, he presents several relations between human beings in order to render man's struggle for existence and affection in a meaningless world. To what an extent this is being accomplished in Beckett's work becomes the main task of this article, the main focus being the universal validity of the human condition and destiny. Thus, these are limited to the ultimate truths of existence and the metaphysical implication of the dramatic discourse. However, the topic of aestheticism being inexhaustible and somehow in the eyes of the perceiver it is a prerogative of the argument to stress out the effect on the reader of the narrative as such and to refer strictly to the human condition viewed in a highly philosophical manner. [1]

Hugh Culik, in "Mathematics as Metaphor: Samuel Beckett and the Esthetics of Incompleteness", discusses how writer Samuel Beckett emerges as a problematic Post-Modernist despite his immersion in the intellectual life of Modernism. It concerns the adequacy and completeness of formal systems, his mathematical

---

[1] Luca I. "The Nothingness in Samuel Beckett's Prose Writing *How It Is* as an Aesthetic Concept". Philologica Jassyensia, 2015, 11(1):199-205.

allusions, written works of Beckett.①

Paul Ardoin, in "Deleuze's Monstrous Beckett: Movement and Paralysis", takes the title of his article "from a 1973 letter in which Gilles Deleuze describes 'the history of philosophy as a kind of buggery' that involves 'getting onto the back of an author, and giving him a child, which would be his and which would at the same time be a monster.' My suggestion is that we keep this in mind when considering Deleuze's engagement with Beckett, particularly as Deleuze becomes increasingly important in Beckett territory. Deleuze's readings of Beckett neglect Beckett's early work—work that demonstrates a parodic engagement with the very idea of Deleuze-esque philosophies of movement and freedom. What Deleuze celebrates as the rhizomatic place where things pick up speed, Beckett describes as 'an unsurveyed marsh of sloth.' I return to Beckett's *More Pricks than Kicks* and *Dream of Fair to Middling Women* to sketch a line between thinking philosophically and the concretion of ideas and method into a philosophy."②

Aislinn O'Donnell, in "Another Relationship to Failure: Reflections on Beckett and Education", argues that "failure is seen as a problem in education. From failing schools, to failing students to rankings of universities, literacy or numeracy, the perception that one has failed to compete or to compare favourably with others has led to a series of policy initiatives internationally designed to ensure 'success for all'. But when success is measured in comparison with others or against benchmarks or standards, then it is impossible to see how all could be successful given the parameters laid down. What are the implications of a culture that values success and achievement? How difficult is it to become the kind of

---

① Culik H. "Mathematics as Metaphor: Samuel Beckett and the Esthetics of Incompleteness". Papers on Language & Literature, 1993, 29(2):131-151.

② Ardoin P. "Deleuze's Monstrous Beckett: Movement and Paralysis". Journal of Modern Literature, 2015, 38(2):134-149.

individual who is flourishing, autonomous and becomes 'all she can be', in particular under the precarious conditions of contemporary capitalism? Samuel Beckett was sceptical of the quest for progress, production and prestige. His philosophy invites another way of thinking about failure, not as something one is, but rather as something one does: the pain and fear of inadequacy that can mark educational relations and experiences is alleviated by a more renunciative, gentle philosophy of education. There are two interwoven strands in this article. One questions the emphasis on competition and achievement in contemporary education and explores its implications for our relationship to failure. The second, strongly influenced by Beckett, explores ways of reimagining our relationship to failure in such a way that allows us to reflect on what matters in life."[1]

Chris Ackerley, in "'Perfection Is Not of This World': Samuel Beckett and Mysticism", argues that "Beckett's agnosticism is offset by a curious and contradictory fascination with the mystical traditions of the Western Middle Ages. Deeply influenced by Thomas à Kempis, Beckett yet remained skeptical: his fictional persona, Belacqua, calls himself a dud mystic, a John of the Crossroads; early intimations are parodic; *Murphy*'s 'necessary journey' is toward an inner darkness; Watt's attempt to 'eff the ineffable' is disastrous; quests in the *Three Novels* and *Texts for Nothing* end in an impasse; and *How It Is* concludes that the impulse toward the light is finally 'all balls.' Even so, elements of mysticism are manifested in such themes as the 'voice' and the 'Not-I'; in touches of gnosticism that inform *Krapp's Last Tape*; in the spectral imagery of 'Ghost Trio'; and in the late 'closed space' prose." These testify to a lasting legacy of mysticism in a major twentieth-century corpus of religious writing.[2]

---

[1] O'Donnell A. "Another Relationship to Failure: Reflections on Beckett and Education". Journal of Philosophy of Education, 2014, 48(2):260-275.

[2] Ackerley C. "'Perfection Is Not of This World': Samuel Beckett and Mysticism". Mystics Quarterly, 2004, 30(1/2):28-55.

Ruben Borg, in "Putting the Impossible to Work: Beckettian Afterlife and the Posthuman Future of Humanity", analyzes "the rhetoric of futurity at work in a number of texts dealing with the 'posthuman future of humanity.' It follows these texts in an attempt to historicize such a future in relation to human history. But it also identifies an overwhelming temporal contradiction at the heart of their discourse: that the posthuman is already with us even as it remains to come. If so, is posthuman identity to be interpreted as a mere phase in the history of human subjectivity? Does posthumanity come about in response to ethical and epistemological challenges inherited from the experience of human subjects? Or is it rather an altogether new paradigm that renders the very use of words like 'subjectivity,' 'history,' and 'experience' anachronistic? Drawing on Hegel, Derrida, and especially Beckett, I argue that an experience of the impossible informs the moment of posthuman self-reflection; and consequently, that the challenge of theorizing a point of contact between human and posthuman being (or human and posthuman history) calls for a new, ad hoc interpretation of the concept of 'impossibility.'"[1]

Aubrey D. Kubiak, in "Godot: The Non-Negative Nothingness", discusses an aspect of "*En Attendant Godot*, a play by Samuel Beckett, an Irish author who wrote in French". Among other issues, the author considers the play in view of Martin Heidegger's conception of nothingness, an examination which leads to a less pessimistic view of the work.[2]

---

[1] Borg R. "Putting the Impossible to Work: Beckettian Afterlife and the Posthuman Future of Humanity". Journal of Modern Literature, 2012, 35(4):163-180.

[2] Kubiak A D. "Godot: The Non-Negative Nothingness". Romance Notes, 2008, 48(3):395-405.

9. Marxism Study

Andy Merrifield, in "Endgame Marxism (and Urbanism)", explores the idea of Beckettian Marxism, a kind of Marxism that can be used to confront endgame urbanism. Topics covered include the Irish writer Samuel Beckett's specialty in claustrophobic confinement, the type of confinement engendered by urban expansion, how Beckett's focus on loss and poverty might be the spirit that the Marxist tradition needs to revive, and the idea of a Marxist Underground with a critical culture that might make cities interesting and democratic again. [1]

10. Psychological Study

Joshua Powell, in "'Of All Things a Face Appeared': Reading Faces in Samuel Beckett's *That Time*", argues that "Samuel Beckett registered a number of ideas regarding the face. He took note of the Gestalt idea that the baby is born with the innate ability to distinguish the figure of a face from a blurry buzzing background. His interest was also piqued by the finding that one's perception of a facial expression might change depending on how much of the face is made visible. These ideas would influence his later work. Focusing on the short play *That Time*, this article looks at Beckett's dramatic presentation of a face alone in the dark. It compares Beckett's approach to face-reading with the study of the face that developed in twentieth-century experimental psychology. Beckett, I suggest, is working with the idea, common in experimental psychology, that facial expressions

---

[1] Merrifield A. "Endgame Marxism (and Urbanism)". Monthly Review: An Independent Socialist Magazine, 2019, 71(6):47-53.

can be produced involuntarily and perceived effortlessly. However, he also draws attention to a more effortful mode of producing and perceiving faces. Finally, the article situates Beckett's portrayal of the face in relation to a modern culture that increasingly recognises—and celebrates—the face's unmanageability, but has not stopped attempting to manage the face."①

Feargal Whelan, in "'No Nation Wanted It So Much': Beckett, Swift and Psychiatric Confinement in Ireland", argues that "Samuel Beckett displays an interest in portraying figures normally regarded as insane within their communities, and who are frequently depicted interacting with institutions of mental care. Taking the representation of three asylums in three separate works, this paper aims to explore a developing and complicated meditation on the subjects of mental health and incarceration by the author. Beckett's recurring reference to Jonathan Swift and the constant presence of sexual anxiety in these narratives allows him to produce a nuanced critique of the development of modes of confinement in the emerging Irish state."②

Kyle Gillette, in "Zen and the Art of Self-Negation in Samuel Beckett's *Not I*", discusses Samuel Beckett's play *Not I* which fleshes out the mental suffering cited by Buddhism as caused by grasping thoughts or sensations and adhering to a delusion of a persistent self. The play in performance establishes a distinctively embodied empty space through which the notion of a subject is radically emptied of intrinsic value. It indicates that Beckett does not promise anything which from a Zen perspective points to the emptiness of forms, sensations and formations.③

---

① Powell J. "'Of All Things a Face Appeared': Reading Faces in Samuel Beckett's *That Time*". Critical Survey, 2015, 27(1):85-101.
② Whelan F. "'No Nation Wanted It So Much': Beckett, Swift and Psychiatric Confinement in Ireland". Estudios Irlandeses, 2019, 14(2): 92-103.
③ Gillette K. "Zen and the Art of Self-Negation in Samuel Beckett's *Not I*". Comparative Drama, 2012, 46(3):283-302.

Codruta Mirela Stanisoara, in "The Absurd of Modern Life—The Interface between Two Different Literary Identities: Samuel Beckett and Octavian Paler", discusses the works of the Irish writer Samuel Beckett and the Romanian writer Octavian Paler. It mentions that Becket's play *Waiting for Godot* is an extraordinary creation due to the emotions created through the plot which becomes a reference for many bodies of works. It notes that Paler's novel *Life on a Platform* is thematically similar to Becket's play, though published in two different periods. It states that both works describe a strong sense of longingness and a desire to escape from another inferno. [1]

Stephen John Dilks, in "Samuel Beckett's Samuel Johnson", discusses how the development of a selective portrait of the author Samuel Johnson by Samuel Beckett helps him begin to articulate his own literary aesthetic: analysis of the period of preparation made by Samuel Johnson which preceeded the period considered by many as the creative turning point for the author; reconstruction of the Samuel Beckett's relationship with James Joyce before and after 1937. [2]

Sarah Gendron, in "'A Cogito for the Dissolved Self': Writing, Presence, and the Subject in the Work of Samuel Beckett, Jacques Derrida, and Gilles Deleuze", presents information on the writing, presence, and the subject in the work of Samuel Beckett, Jacques Derrida, and Gilles Deleuze. Beckett, Derrida and Deleuze evoke elements of traditional narrative and of the self in order ultimately to problematize any beliefs one might have about narrative and about the writing/written subject. From their work, one learns that the self is capable of producing text, but it is in turn subject to being produced by text, even, in the end, reduced to nothing more than text itself. *Of Grammatology* is Derrida's major

---

[1] Stanisoara C M. "The Absurd of Modern Life—The Interface between Two Different Literary Identities: Samuel Beckett and Octavian Paler". Philologica Jassyensia, 2008, 4(2):217-220.

[2] Dilks S J. "Samuel Becket's Samuel Johnson". Modern Language Review, 2003, 98(2):285-298.

work on the history and status of writing in Western civilization. It is here that he challenges the long held speech/writing power structure. Though many scholars have noted Beckett's continual allusions to Descartes's method of forming the subject through the employment of systematic doubt, the results Beckett's characters get after using this method are dramatically different from those of Descartes.[①]

Ila Ahlawat, in "Tracing the Mother to the Daughter, the Self to the Image: Separation Anxiety in Beckett's *Footfalls*", focuses on the allure of the maternal, a metapresence in Samuel Beckett's play *Footfalls*. The article examines the pre-Oedipal role of the mother into shaping the vocal and kinetic rhythms of her daughter. There is a detailed discussion on the force that steers the daughter towards the mother and vice versa and how this force resists the spectacular matricide that the audience longs to commit on the theatrical space. This piece will seek to trace the play of the incestuous auditory and visual intimacy between May, pacing up and down the wooden plank, and her mother. The article also discusses the tendencies of a defensive narcissism in these women that is gratifying, a natural consequence of pathogenic repression and concealment, and symbolizes plenitude and plurality.[②]

11. Narratology Study

Rick de Villiers, in "A Defense of Wretchedness: *Molloy* and Humiliation", argues that Beckett warned against the neatness of identification. Yet the dangers of conflation are often courted—both in the fictional worlds themselves where suffering

---

① Gendron S. "'A Cogito for the Dissolved Self': Writing, Presence, and the Subject in the Work of Samuel Beckett, Jacques Derrida, and Gilles Deleuze". Journal of Modern Literature, 2004, 28(1): 47-64.

② Ahlawat I. "Tracing the Mother to the Daughter, the Self to the Image: Separation Anxiety in Beckett's Footfalls". Sexuality & Culture, 2017, 21(3): 651-663.

is at a constant, and also in the sometimes overly-familiar narratives of surrounding scholarship. Given this conflict, how does humiliation—and responses to it—define Beckett's individual "creatures"? In *Molloy*, despite the many likenesses between the title character and his near-doppelgänger, humiliation manifests as an ontologically determining phenomenon that disallows the conflation and consolidation of private suffering. Alongside the many instances of wretchedness and abuse, the novel quietly posits humility as ethical imperative when approaching the suffering of others. [1]

Edward D. Miller, in "The Performance of Listening: Samuel Beckett's *That Time*", presents a critique of the play *That Time*, written by Samuel Beckett, as well as the film adaptation of the play directed by Charles Garrad, focusing on ways in which it can be analyzed through aspects of performance theory. The author argues that Beckett should be classified as not only a playwright and novelist, but also a writer of performance media due to his constructions of the characters found in *That Time*. The article overviews the plot of the play, discusses the concept of auscultation, and comments on additional plays by Beckett including *Not I* and *Krapp's Last Tape*. [2]

Tomasz Wisniewski, in "Space and Communication in Samuel Beckett's *Company* and in Some of His Dramatic Works", concentrate on the relationship between space and communication in his selected works (the narrative—*Company*, radio plays, films as well as stage plays) so as to show that *Company* contributes to the understanding of main semantic concerns (i. e. darkness vs. light, inside vs. outside, stage vs. theatre, speaking vs. silence, monologue vs. dialogue, mimetic vs. metaphoric, vertical vs. horizontal etc.) in Beckett's drama. The article also

---

[1] De Villers R. "A Defense of the Wretchedness: *Molloy* and Humiliation". Journal of Modern Literature, 2019, 42(4):93-110.
[2] Miller E D. "The Performance of Listening: Samuel Beckett's *That Time*". Cinema Journal, 2012, 51(3):150-155.

focuses on the invariant principles constructing the model of the world that emerges from all the works in question. The author places observation in the context of English language criticism on Samuel Beckett.[①]

Paul A. Harris, in "Thinking on Different Levels of Narrative Time: J. T. Fraser's Eotemporal Hierarchical Theory and Samuel Beckett's Prototemporal Cosmos", examines "different modes of organizing narrative time and the thinking about time that narrative temporalities make possible. J. T. Fraser's hierarchical theory of time is framed as a narrative which displays a conflict between subsuming time into form and depicting a natural history of time. Fraser's work is characterized by an eotemporal narrative time that is able to range freely across a continuous, reversible temporal world. Fraser's assessment of Samuel Beckett's plays as depicting a prototemporal cosmos is summarized and then supplemented with reflections on how the prototemporal narrative time of *Waiting for Godot* enables thought to confront time, death and life in stark clarity."[②]

Paul Shanks, in "The Unnamed Itinerant in Samuel Beckett's Novellas and James Kelman's *Lean Tales*", focuses on the works of Samuel Beckett, a literary father in journalistic and academic discussion of James Kelman's fiction. The author states that in comparison of the two writers, it appears that Beckett has adopted the solitary and no political significance of Kelman's work. Both writers use a narrative voice that is penetrated by doubt and the acute awareness of instability between utterance and the transcription of utterance marked by performance.[③]

---

① Wisniewski T. "Space and Communication in Samuel Beckett's *Company* and in Some of His Dramatic Works". Impulso, 2006, 17(42):29-41.

② Harris P A. "Thinking on Different Levels of Narrative Time: J. T. Fraser's Eotemporal Hierarchical Theory and Samuel Beckett's Prototemporal Cosmos". KronoScope, 2013, 13(2):203-216.

③ Shanks P. "The Unnamed Itinerant in Samuel Beckett's Novellas and James Kelman's *Lean Tales*". Scottish Studies Review, 2008, 9(2):109-127.

Graley Herren, in "Facing the Darkness: Interrogations across Genre in Samuel Beckett's *What Where*", traces the transformation of *What Where* from a stage play into a teleplay to witness Samuel Beckett's refinement of his own themes: characters of the play; literary works that are considered important by Beckett and are reflected in the play *What Where*; challenges faced by Beckett in textual revisions of the play *What Where*. ①

Nathaniel Davis, in "'Not a Soul in Sight!': Beckett's Fourth Wall", argues that while the theatrical device of "breaking the fourth wall" has come to be seen as a characteristic technique of modernist theater, it is not often associated with the plays of Samuel Beckett—perhaps the quintessential modernist playwright. While Beckett employs the device in some of his early plays—most markedly in the lesser-known Eleutheria—he eventually moves away from anything resembling the "alienation effect" (as theorized by Bertolt Brecht), in which the fourth-wall break asserts the supremacy of objective reality over that of the dramatic fiction. In rejecting Brecht's methodology, Beckett does not, however, return to a naturalist theatrical model. In the "failed realism" of his most successful plays, *Waiting for Godot* and *Endgame*, Beckett's nuanced treatment of the fourth wall helps to present the stage as a space of complete ontological indeterminacy, reflecting the unstable metaphysics of lived experience. ②

Emily C. Bloom, in "'The Protestant Thing to Do': Anglo-Irish Performance in James Joyce's *Dubliners* and Samuel Beckett's *All That Fall*", examines Samuel Beckett's radio play *All That Fall* and the book *Dubliners* by James Joyce, which both predict the performative nature of Protestant identity in Ireland. She argues that Joyce and Beckett specifically target Irish revival drama for perpetuating

---

① Herren G. "Facing the Darkness: Interrogations across Genre in Samuel Beckett's *What Where*". Midwest Quarterly, 2002, 43(3):322-336.

② Davis N. "'Not a Soul in Sight!': Beckett's Fourth Wall". Journal of Modern Literature, 2015, 38(2):86-102.

representational inequities between Catholics and Protestants in Ireland. She compares *Dubliners* to *All That Fall* to show the extent to which both works explore the politics of the revival stage, metropolitan Anglo-Irish identity and sectarian divisions in pre- and post-Independence Ireland. She concludes that both Joyce and Beckett, through their explorations of Anglo-Irish performativity, have reinvented narrative forms in their use and abuse of dramatic staging. [1]

Peter Boxall, in "Blind Seeing: Deathwriting from Dickinson to the Contemporary", traces a tradition of what is here called "deathwriting" as it stretches from Emily Dickinson, to Franz Kafka, to Samuel Beckett, to Cormac McCarthy. The works of all these writers, the essay argues, are driven by the urge to give a poetic form to the experience of death, to make death thinkable and narratable. Alongside this tradition of deathwriting, and interwoven with it, one can discern too, a fascination with "blind seeing", an attempt to make darkness visible, or to overcome the distinction between the light and the dark, the visible and the invisible. In reading the connection between deathwriting and blind seeing as it runs from Dickinson to the contemporary, the essay argues that these writers allow us to glimpse a differently constituted relationship between the living and the dead, and between the perceptible and the imperceptible. At a contemporary moment, when it has become urgent to rethink our apparatuses for world picturing, with the emergence of the Anthropocene as a critical context for all of our imaginings, the essay offers this history of deathwriting as a radically different way of seeing, without the aid of human light. [2]

Dirk Van Hulle, in "Hesitancy in Joyce's and Beckett's Manuscripts", investigates the notion of hesitancy in the works and manuscripts of James Joyce and

---

[1] Bloom E C. "'The Protestant Thing to Do': Anglo-Irish Performance in James Joyce's *Dubliners* and Samuel Beckett's *All That Fall*". Texas Studies in Literature & Language, 2009, 51(1):1-16.

[2] Boxall P. "Blind Seeing: Deathwriting from Dickinson to the Contemporary". New Formations, 2017(89/90):192-211.

Samuel Beckett. In the book *Finnegans Wake* by Joyce, the metafictional ways in which a text can draw attention to the underlying grid instead of hiding the traces of the writing process are exemplified. However, in *Stirrings Still* by Beckett, hesitancy is said to be notable in the early stages of the writing process. It is also noted that hesitancy in Beckett's manuscripts is not a sign of incertitude, but a carefully introduced motif illustrated in the genesis of *Krapp's Last Tape*. [1]

12. Cultural Study

Christopher Morrison, in "The Wandering Jew in Samuel Beckett's *Waiting for Godot*", suggests that Beckett uses at least three disparate versions of the legend to derive much of the raw material in *Waiting for Godot*. A good deal of the two vagabonds' dialogue may be derived from the generic myth of the Jewish carpenter whom, the day of the Crucifixion, Christ damned to a miserable life wandering the earth until the Second Coming. But the pair's predicament also fits perfectly with a little known version of the myth from *Podolia* (*Ukraine*) published as an annotation in English by Avrahm Yarmolinsky in 1929. "Furthermore, important elements of Lucky's character may have been derived from *Le Juif Errant, trois acts, prologue et intermède* (1946), by the relatively unknown Alsatian surrealist Maxime Alexandre (1899-1976). Alexandre portrays Jews as bearing a heavy burden for mankind as guardians of humanity and of higher aesthetics, who will (exactly like Lucky) under no circumstances put down their heavy load. Although the origins of the myth are anti-Semitic, this reading appears to underline Beckett's reputation as

---

[1] Van Hulle D. "Hesitancy in Joyce's and Beckett's Manuscripts". Texas Studies in Literature & Language, 2009, 51(1):17-27.

a philo-semite."①

Yael Levin, in "Beckett's Path of Least Resistance: Attention, Distraction, Drift", utilizes Beckett's fictional and critical explorations of attention, distraction and drift to reflect on the ways in which, stripped of the conventions of cultural production, walking, thinking and artistic endeavor might be reimagined outside the normative scripts of biopolitics. Centralized and teleological forms give way to rhizomatic instantiations of the same in a process pertaining to all three registers at once (walking, thinking and writing). The result is the formation of a gesture that though suggestive of resistance cannot be viewed as such, in so far as it eschews negation. The author traces a movement from the dialectical oscillation of attention and distraction in Proust to Beckett's fashioning of an alternative that finds expression not only in the abstractions of thought and language but also in embodied experience. This alternative will be termed "drift", a label denoting neither principle nor concept, but a mode of being that anticipates our attempts to think the human in the sensory digital present. Beckett's experiments allow us to reconsider forms of knowledge, understanding and conditioning. No less significant is his lesson on how we might do so without becoming embroiled in the dialectics of resistance and compliance.②

13. Canonization

S. E. Gontarski, in "Revising Himself: Performance as Text in Samuel Beckett's Theatre", focuses on Samuel Beckett's transformation from playwright to

---

① Morrison C. "The Wandering Jew in Samuel Beckett's *Waiting for Godot*". Journal of Modern Jewish Studies, 2012, 11(3):399-417.
② Levin Y. "Beckett's Path of Least Resistance: Attention, Distraction, Drift". Estudios Irlandeses, 2019, 14(2):38-51.

theatrical artist: concern for a standard of fidelity in the staging of his plays from the start of his career; discovery of theater; impact on his writing; self-collaboration as author and director. ①

Sean McCarthy, in "Giving Sam a Second Life: Beckett's Plays in the Age of Convergent Media", explores how media practice is changing texts ascribed to traditional literary or theatrical genres, particularly in the plays by Samuel Beckett. It examines Henry Jenkins's theory of convergence to help contextualize the exploration of Beckett in the complex media culture of 2008. It suggests that virtual environments, such as Second Life, offer productive possibilities to engage with the texts of Beckett in the twenty-first century. It explores Beckett's play *Eh Joe*, as an example of his convergent art. ②

14. Ethical Study

Ben Ware, in "Tragic-Dialectical-Perfectionism: On the Ethics of Beckett's *Endgame*", explores the ethical dimensions of Samuel Beckett's *Endgame*, in spite of—indeed, because of—the play's apparent negation of all positive talk of human value and community. In the first part of the paper, the author examines Stanley Cavell's suggestion, putting forward in his Carus Lectures of 1988, that Beckett's play can be read as a work that embodies and develops the idea of Emersonian moral perfectionism. In part two, the author turns the tables somewhat. After demarcating some of the social limits of Cavell's ethical outlook, the author then asks what it might mean to rediscover perfectionism in a more politicized form,

---

① Gontarski S E. "Revising Himself: Performance as Text in Samuel Beckett's Theatre". Journal of Modern Literature, 1998, 22(1):131.
② McCarthy S. "Giving Sam a Second Life: Beckett's Plays in the Age of Convergent Media". Texas Studies in Literature & Language, 2009, 51(1):102-117.

something that the author attempts to do via an exploration of the tragic dimensions of Beckett's play. While retaining some important features of Cavell's "thematics of perfectionism", this approach aims at the same time to move beyond it in order to grasp how *Endgame* might, in Beckett's own words, provide an inkling of the terms in which our condition is to be thought again.[①]

Suzanne Dow, in "Beckett's Humour, from an Ethics of Finitude to an Ethics of the Real", explores the ethics of Samuel Beckett's humour. It takes issue with the dominant reading of Beckettian humour as the redemption of a negativity occasioned by humanity's finitude. The paradigmatic case in point is here taken to be Simon Critchley's account, wherein ethics is cast as a process of coming to terms with disappointment ensuing from the inaccessibility of the Kantian Thing-in-Itself. This article takes up a Lacanian psychoanalytic perspective to recast Beckett's humour as, far from offering solace for finitude, highlighting instead the excess or remainder that insists, and resists philosophy's attempts to sublate it into a version of the Good. As such, the ethical demand evoked by Beckettian humour is not the attenuation of the disappointing lack implied by finitude, but rather a coping with the egregious excess of inhuman infinitude.[②]

---

① Ware B. "Tragic-Dialectical-Perfectionism: On the Ethics of Beckett's *Endgame*". College Literature, 2015, 42(1):3-22.
② Dow S. "Beckett's Humour, from an Ethics of Finitude to an Ethics of the Real". Paragraph: A Journal of Modern Critical Survey, 2011, 34(1):121-136.

Chapter 7

Harrold Pinter

Harrold Pinter(1930-2008)

Harold Pinter was one of the most gifted playwrights to come out of the 1950s and 1960s. For over 50 years, he has written prolifically on various subjects. His major thematic concern is with people's internal fabric of fears, desires, guilt, and sexual drives that debilitate and jeopardize their chances of survival. His major works include *The Room*, *The Birthday Party*, and *The Homecoming*.

Critical Perspectives

1. Post-colonial Study

Rebecca Dyer, in "Class and Anticolonial Politics in Harold Pinter and Joseph Losey's *The Servant*", argues that "Critics of *The Servant* based on the 1948 novel by Robin Maugham, have not examined the London-set films many allusions to the global South. However, the screenwriters and directors archives as well as many aspects of the film—including wardrobe, set design, music, and dialogue—reveal the significance of these references. Departing from Maugham's novel, Pinter and Losey portray the master as an African plantation owner's son with a plan to 'clear the jungle' in Brazil. These additions to the narrative connect domestic servitude and abuses of power within Britain to the international division of labor established during colonial conquest and align the film's class commentary with the anticolonial movements underway in the 1960s."[①]

2. Philosophical Study

Merve Aydoğdu, in "An Althusserian Reading of Harold Pinter's *One for the Road*", argues that Louis Althusser in his seminal essay *Ideology and Ideological State Apparatuses* in *Lenin and Philosophy and Other Essays* (1970) discusses the

---

① Dyer R. "Class and Anticolonial Politics in Harold Pinter and Joseph Losey's *The Servant*". Journal of Modern Literature, 2015, 38(4):147-167.

ways through which a State dominates/subjugates its subjects by means of Repressive and Ideological State Apparatuses, the effects of which are traceable in Harold Pinter's 1984 play *One for the Road*. Within this scope, this paper seeks to examine Pinter's one-act play from an Althusserian point of view with a view to demonstrating the manipulative influence of ISAs and SA on the creation of subjects who would serve for the State. [1]

Alina Elena Roşca, in "Multi-levelled Representations of Power in Harold Pinter's Plays", argues that the concept of power disposes of multiple representations in Harold Pinter's plays: at the level of language, where characters evade communication, at the level of spatiality, where characters appropriate selectively and differently the scenic objects and space, at the level of memory, where subjectivity allows characters to isolate themselves and preserve their position, at the level of gender representations, where characters abuse the preconceived beliefs in order to impose their own values. Using all the vehicles that are at their disposal, discursive and non-discursive, characters engage in power-struggles, because they refuse to reveal their own identity and to be overwhelmed by fears and insecurities. When there is a menacing situation/ person threatening their apparent stable world, their anxieties and frustrations come to the surface. [2]

3. Feminism Study

Alina Elena Roşca, in "Mimicking Subjection to the Name-of-the-Father in Harold Pinter's *The Homecoming*", embraces the postulation that feminine

---

[1] Aydoġdu M. "An Althusserian Reading of Harold Pinter's *One for the Road*". Journal of History, Culture & Art Research, 2014, 3(1):1-11.
[2] Roşca A E. "Multi-levelled Representations of Power in Harold Pinter's Plays". Petroleum-Gas University of Ploiesti Bulletin Philology Series, 2009, 61(2):91-98.

sexuality and physicality displays its movement in its own distinct space of manifestation. Female corporality lives outside the predominant ideological representations of patriarchy which can no longer impose their structures or prove their efficiency. In Harold Pinter's *The Homecoming*, femininity involves in mimicry. Imitation of the conventional roles women occupy in the politics of masculinity implies mimicking subordination to the Name-of-the-Father. Paradoxically, this type of imitation allows women to disrupt and display the fabricated nature of the ideological apparatus in which they operate.[①]

4. Narratology Study

Emil Roy, in "G. B. Shaw's *Heartbreak House* and Harold Pinter's *The Homecoming*: Comedies of Implosion", exploits the lasting archetype deeply rooted in the dramatic form. It shows in both plays the dichotomized parent/spousal figures project infantile confusion toward parent figures between nurturing, protective images and threatening, intimidating symbols.[②]

Tony Hammond, in "Midrash on Goldberg", argues that the character of Goldberg in Harold Pinter's earliest major play, *The Birthday Party*, presents an important challenge to us to question his claim to represent Jewishness and instead to understand him as a destructive stereotype of the Jew and Jewishness. This is a challenge which has by and large not been taken up by critics. Goldberg, like Shylock and Fagin and others in the canon of English literature, is a complex, intentionally villainous, but colourful and memorable figure, who, against the

---

① Roşca A E. "Mimicking Subjection to the Name-of-the-Father in Harold Pinter's *The Homecoming*". Word & Text: A Journal of Literary Studies & Linguistics, 2011, 1(1):92-99.

② Roy E. "G. B. Shaw's *Heartbreak House* and Harold Pinter's *The Homecoming*: Comedies of Implosion". Comparative Drama, 2007, 41(3):335-348.

relative paucity of other images of Jews and Jewishness, comes to stand for the Jew and reinforce essentially antisemitic stereotypes, even among those who explicitly reject the prejudice. The undefined sense of threat and violence, which from the outset of Pinter's oeuvre has remained a dominant feature, in this play finds some measure of definition through an examination of the character Goldberg, and we can see how destructive stereotypes of our identity held by others, and sustained often by the inattention of the majority, are the fertile soil of violent persecution and cruelty. Created just over a decade after the opening of the death camps, Pinter's Goldberg shows the spectre did not perish with the people. [1]

Herb Greer, in "Down and out in London", focuses on dramatist Harold Pinter. Pinter's flair as a dramatist is impressive. He discovers that the conversation can be emphasized and given apparent meaning by introducing arbitrary pauses among the dialogue lines. Pinter is known as a theatrical guru, whose work reveals the depths of human experience, life and death. During the 1960s, Pinter's association with a stage work was enough to ensure respectful attention. *Ashes to Ashes* is the latest work of Pinter as of June 1997. It contains cryptic hints about marital cruelty and political oppression. There is no trace of humor in the play. [2]

Theodore Dalrymple, in "Reticence or Insincerity, Rattigan or Pinter", focuses on the life and works of British theater persons Terence Rattigan and Harold Pinter: quality of plays made by Rattigan; criticisms faced by Rattigan for the quality of his plays; personal life of Rattigan; reasons for the popularity of Pinter's plays as compared to Rattigan's plays; contribution of Pinter to the cultural change in theater. [3]

---

[1] Hammond T. "Midrash on Goldberg". European Judaism, 2014, 47(2):41-49.
[2] Greer H. "Down and Out in London". National Review, 1997, 49(12):52-53.
[3] Dalrymple T. "Reticence or Insincerity, Rattigan or Pinter". New Criterion, 2000, 19(3):12-20.

5. Biographical Study

Michael Karwowski, in "Harold Pinter 1930-2008—A Tale of Two Lives", discusses phases in the career of playwright Harold Pinter. The author comments that Pinter ceases to write plays in favor of promoting anti-American propaganda. He suggests that Pinter espouses no political viewpoints in plays such as *The Birthday Party*, *The Homecoming* and *The Caretaker*, but instead focuses on the relationship of reality to illusion.[①]

John Lahr, in "Demolition Man", discusses the life and work of playwright Harold Pinter with a particular focus on his play *The Homecoming*. Pinter comments on his interest in language, especially with regard to his use of language in *The Homecoming*, and reflects on his career. Pinter's public image and political activity are also discussed. The author relates details of his own relationship with Pinter and his writing.[②]

Jay Parini, in "Pinter's Plays, Pinter's Politics", focuses on discussions related to British playwright Harold Pinter, the Nobel Prize winner in Literature. Columnist Christopher Hitchens criticizes that the award to someone who gives up literature for politics decades ago, and whose politics are primitive and hysterically anti-American and pro-dictatorial, is part of the almost complete degradation of the Nobel racket. There can be no doubt about Pinter's anti-imperial politics. Of course the Nobel committee in Stockholm is hardly above making their choices on political grounds. From the right, in particular, the American reaction to the Pinter

---

① Karwowski M. "Harold Pinter 1930-2008—A Tale of Two Lives". Contemporary Review, 2009, 291(1693): 226-236.

② Lahr J. "Demolition Man". The New Yorker, 2007, 83(41):54-69.

award has been one of outrage.[①]

6. Reception Study

Paul Hoggart, in "In on the Joke", discusses the success of playwright Harold Pinter's work in mainstream Broadway theater as of January 2014, despite his polarizing political views and complex narrative structures. Topics discussed include the production of his plays *Betrayal*, starring Daniel Craig, and *No Man's Land*, starring Sir Ian McKellen and Sir Patrick Stewart.[②]

7. Ethical Study

Joseph Hynes, in "Pinter and Morality", discusses the aspects of morality in the plays of Harold Pinter: the moral life there is to be derived from a number of his most renowned plays; questions about what his plays consist of; the influence of existentialism; how he is eminently anti-sentimental and anti-nostalgic; his plays.[③]

8. Comparative Study

Peter L. Hays and Stephanie Tucker, in "No Sanctuary: Hemingway's *The Killers* and Pinter's *The Birthday Party*", discusses the influence of writer Ernest

---

① Parini J. "Pinter's Plays, Pinter's Politics". Chronicle of Higher Education, 2005, 52(12):15.
② Hoggart P. "In on the Joke". Newsweek Global, 2014, 162(3):120-126.
③ Hynes J. "Pinter and Morality". Virginia Quarterly Review, 1992, 68(4):740-752.

Hemingway on playwright Harold Pinter: confession of Pinter regarding his readings of the works of Hemingway; similarities between the short story *The Killers* by Hemingway and the play *The Birthday Party* by Pinter; personal similarities of the two writers. ①

---

① Hays P L, Tucker S. "No Sanctuary: Hemingway's *The Killers* and Pinter's *The Birthday Party*". Papers on Language & Literature, 1985, 21(4):417-424.

Chapter 8

Tom Stoppard

Tom Stoppard(1937-)

Tom Stoppard, as the successor of the absurd drama of the older generation such as Samuel Beckett and Eugene Ionesco (1912-1994), wrote to continue it in his own manner in the English theater. His play, *Rosencrantz and Guildenstern Are Dead* (1967), made his name as an absurd dramatist. It was the point at which he steadily climbed to the peak of his absurd dramatist career in the 1970s.

Critical Perspectives

1. Thematic Study

Wynn Wheldon, in "Tom Stoppard's Great Jewish Play", offers information about Tom Stoppard's play, *Leopoldstadt*, which opens at Wyndham's Theatre in London and concerns the fates of two haute bourgeois Viennese families in the period from 1899 to 1955. Topics include reports that lectures begin to reveal the extent of his Jewishness, a self-discovery that leads directly to *Leopoldstadt* decades later.[1]

Joseph Hynes, in "Tom Stoppard's Lighted March", discusses the play *Rosencrantz and Guildenstern Are Dead*, by Tom Stoppard: insistence of the play that art is life, illusion is reality; underlying of the play's plot in determinism versus free will; comparison of the play by Stoppard with *Hamlet*, by William Shakespeare; excerpt from the play *Rosencrantz and Guildenstern Are Dead*.[2]

2. Biographical Study

Carlo Vareschi, in "Fear and Loathing in Prague: Tom Stoppard's *Cahoot's Macbeth*", offers the author's insights regarding *Dogg's Hamlet*, *Cahoot's Macbeth*, two plays written by playwright Tom Stoppard to be performed together.

---

[1] Wheldon W. "Tom Stoppard's Great Jewish Play". Commentary, 2020, 149(4):51-54.

[2] Hynes J. "Tom Stoppard's Lighted March". Virginia Quarterly Review, 1995, 71(4):642-655.

Topics include the Czechoslovakian roots of Stoppard, the character of a Czech Jewish child named Jan in the plays, and the premiere of *Dogg's Hamlet, Cahoot's Macbeth* at the Arts Center of the University of Warwick on May 21, 1979.①

Ira B. Nadel, in "Writing the Life of 'Tom Stoppard'", presents a biographical account of playwright Tom Stoppard and of biographical techniques. In writing the life of Tom Stoppard, the biographer has "discovered two subjects: the 'Practical Stoppard,' an empirically minded dramatist, and the man of uncertain identity who might be labeled 'Practically Stoppard.' This latter phrase can mean several things: an admission that the biographer has nearly, but not quite, pinned down his subject, the adverb marking the incomplete nature of the work matching Stoppard's own view of the limitations of biography. Or, it can mean that Stoppard in person is almost, but not exactly, 'Stoppard' the dramatist, the persona of the writer as a dazzling wordsmith differing from the individual who emerged from a series of personal identities."②

3. Narratology Study

William W. Demastes, in "Tom Stoppard's Big Picture: The Chaos that Is Our World", argues that Tom Stoppard's very active utilization of science in many of his plays has resulted in his work—especially the quantum mechanics-informed *Hapgood* and the chaotics-informed *Arcadia*—being held up as paradigmatic of one science/art position or another. Often, critical approaches to these plays involve a

---

① Vareschi C. "Fear and Loathing in Prague: Tom Stoppard's *Cahoot's Macbeth*". Comparative Drama, 2018, 52(1/2):123-139.
② Nadel I B. "Writing the Life of 'Tom Stoppard'". Journal of Modern Literature, 2004, 27(3): 19-29.

checklist of scientific facts, implying that the goal of such art is to serve as a delivery device for scientific breakthroughs. While plays, novels, and movies of various sorts may have such goals in mind, Stoppard's plays do not comfortably fill that agenda, critical arguments to the contrary notwithstanding. Neither do Stoppard's plays show particular interest in engaging any debate about the superiority of one culture over the other. In his two "science plays" in particular, what Stoppard offers is an enrichment of both science and art through metaphorical intertwinings that suggest experience is best served when both camps collaborate. The bigger picture that results argues an overlap in epistemology, namely revealing the uncanny similarity in which artist and scientist approach the material that is our universe. ①

William W. Demastes, in "Portrait of an Artist as Proto-Chaotician: Tom Stoppard Working His Way to Arcadia", presents on the professional career of British playwright Tom Stoppard. It highlights the works of Stoppard from the 1960s to 1980s including Arcadia and Rosencrantz and Guildenstern Are Dead. It states that Stoppard was a proto-chaotician who discovered chaos theory when he wrote Arcadia in the 1980s. ②

Oleg B. Zaslavskii, in "The Little in a Non-Euclidean World: On the Artistic Space in Tom Stoppard's Film and Play Rosencrantz and Guildenstern Are Dead", shows that quite different aspects of Tom Stoppard's work—spatial organization, relationship between reality and the conditional character of events, causality and narrative links, the problems of choice and personality—are united by the spatial one-sided model like the Möbius strip or Klein bottle. The artistic space turns out to be not orientable, the time being cyclic. This enables us to explain the mutual

---

① Demastes W. W. "Tom Stoppard's Big Picture: The Chaos that Is Our World". Interdisciplinary Science Reviews, 2014, 39(3):204-212.

② Demastes WW. "Portrait of an Artist as Proto-Chaotician: Tom Stoppard Working His Way to Arcadia". Narrative, 2011, 19(2):229-240.

exchange of names between Rosencrantz and Guildenstern and a number of other paradoxical features in the plot and composition. The model like the Möbius strip embodies the absence of a free choice: there is no other side in the world and there is no chance to escape from the fate indicated in the title of Tom Stoppard's work. The relevance of topology, e. g. the property of a global nature, is connected with the fact that a bearer of danger is the world as a whole. Apart from this, it points to the fact that such a structure of the world is essentially "non-Euclidean" and cannot be understood on the basis of observations from every-day life or "obvious" experiments like those carried out by Rosencrantz. [1]

4. Cultural Study

Richard Rankin Russell, in "'It Will Make Us Friends': Cultural Reconciliation in Tom Stoppard's *Indian Ink*", comments on the works of playwright Tom Stoppard with special focus on *Indian Ink*. Stoppard was born in the Czech Republic and grew up in Singapore, India, and England. His global origins have inspired a fascination with national identities, particularly the ways in which these identities are interrelated. In his drama *Indian Ink*, he suggests the promise and possibility of cultural reconciliation between English and Indian characters across two generations. Through depicting a series of aesthetic interchanges between the past and the present, Stoppard demonstrates how these processes can heal the distrust fostered by decades of English colonial rule in India. [2]

---

    [1] Zaslavskii O B. "The Little in a Non-Euclidean World: On the Artistic Space in Tom Stoppard's Film and Play *Rosencrantz and Guildenstern Are Dead*". Sign Systems Studies, 2005, 33(2):343-367.
    [2] Russell R R. "'It Will Make Us Friends': Cultural Reconciliation in Tom Stoppard's *Indian Ink*". Journal of Modern Literature, 2004, 27(3):1-18.

Erica Wagner, in "Time Is Short, Life Is Short. There's a Lot to Know", focuses on dramatists Tom Stoppard and his theatrical production *The Hard Problem* at the Dorfman Theatre in London, England. Topics include his receipt of the Writers Guild of America Screen Laurel Award, his authorship of the screenplay for the award-winning film *Shakespeare in Love*, and his thoughts on popular culture in 2015. ①

5. Post-Modernism

Kersti Tarien Powell, in "'Dualism Is the Word': Wave/Particle Functions in Banville and Stoppard", presents on the works of modern-day authors John Banville and Tom Stoppard, who analyze the understanding of British and Irish post-modernism and the association of postmodernism to quantum theory. Topics discussed include Banville's science tetralogy *Doctor Copernicus* (1976), Stoppard's first science play *Hapgood* (1988), and the author's argument that both initially engaged with quantum mechanical ideas but finally turned away from postmodern uncertainty and disconnection. ②

Michael Roeschlein, in "Theatrical Iteration in Stoppard's *Arcadia*: Fractal Mapping, Eternal Recurrence Perichoresis", explores the theatrical iteration in British playwright Tom Stoppard's *Arcadia*. It discusses the theory of deterministic chaos and Stoppard's treatment of dramatic structure, dialogue, character development and audience reception. It indicates that Stoppard constructs *Arcadia*

---

① Wagner E. "Time Is Short, Life Is Short. There's a Lot to Know". New Statesman, 2/6/2015: 26-31.
② Tarien Powell K. "'Dualism Is the Word': Wave/Particle Functions in Banville and Stoppard". Texas Studies in Literature & Language, 2014, 56(3):326-347.

fractally, distorting together postmodernism and spirituality in an elusive alliance.[①]

6. Philosophical Study

Corey Abel, in "The Drama of Politics and Science: Stoppard's *Hapgood*", examines the political play *Hapgood* of Tom Stoppard. It notes that the problematic relationship between science and morality has traditionally been one of determinism versus freedom or reductionism versus meaning. The play explores the impact of the science of subatomic physics on our self-understanding. A brief overview of the play is given. The play rises far beyond the sophistries of popularized physics, not by finding any moral certainty but by evoking the complexities of morality.[②]

7. Performing Art

Herbert F. Tucker, in "History Played Back: In Defense of Stoppard's *Coast of Utopia*", informs that two and a half years ago, "Tom Stoppard's expensive, rewarding trilogy *The Coast of Utopia* concluded, at the National Theatre in London under Trevor Nunn's direction, an initial run that must be regarded as definitive. Demanding dozens of actors in scores of roles, elaborate period costumes by the gross, and a range of settings from Russian country house to West End slum and from Baltic to Mediterranean vistas, this strongly knit three-part script will not travel easily to other venues. Nor will it often find audiences as willing as London's

---

① Roeschlein M. "Theatrical Iteration in Stoppard's *Arcadia*: Fractal Mapping, Eternal Recurrence Perichoresis". Religion & Literature, 2012, 44(3):57-85.

② Abel C. "The Drama of Politics and Science: Stoppard's *Hapgood*". Perspectives on Political Science, 2006, 35(3):143-148.

proved to sit out the nine hours' playing time and absorb the radical nineteenth-century Russian thought that Stoppard has placed, with honorable insistence, at the center of interest. New Yorkers will get to see this work in a somewhat adapted version, as a production has been announced for this year at Lincoln Center, directed by Jack O'Brien. While the invigorating quality of the political debate in Stoppard's trilogy makes production in Washington or Moscow an event devoutly to be wished, the dreary quality of the political debate now evident in both capitals militates pretty decisively against it."①

Terry Teachout, in "Utopians on Stage", discusses the popular success of the play *The Coast of Utopia*, written by Tom Stoppard and starring a famous cast that includes Julia Roberts and Kevin Spacey. The author suggests that the play's success can be attributed to its big names and extensive coverage in the newspaper *The New York Times*.②

8. Psychoanalytical Study

Malcolm Macmillan, in "Alexander the Great, the Dahlia, and the Tortoise", argues that some of the problems of establishing the cause of the death of Alexander the Great are like the attempts to find causes other than hysteria for Anna O.'s symptoms. The more general problem of using plausibility as a criterion of the truth of such reconstructions are illustrated by the arguments embedded in Tom Stoppard's *Arcadia*.③

---

① Tucker H F. "History Played Back: In Defense of Stoppard's *Coast of Utopia*". Raritan, 2005, 24(4):149-169.

② Teachout T. "Utopians on Stage". Commentary, 2007, 123(4):62-65.

③ Macmillan M. "Alexander the Great, the Dahlia, and the Tortoise". Journal of the History of the Neurosciences, 2004, 13(2):150-152.

Chapter 9

Caryl Churchill

Caryl Churchill(1938-   )

For more than thirty years, Caryl Churchill has been combining social commitment with theatrical experimentation. Rarely in modern British drama has the combination been so fruitful. Her play-writing career began in the 1960s, producing numerous acclaimed stage plays, and from the 1990s, moved more and more into a mixed theatre of text, dance, and music. In other words, Churchill has traversed the dramatic spectrum, from word and sound alone in her radio plays, to a greater and greater emphasis on space and movement in her more recent works.

Churchill's dramaturgy is above all the staging of desire, and more particularly the desires of those members of society who are least able to realize them.

Critical Perspectives

1. Gender Study

Sarah DeGeorge, in "'From Bugger to Bragger': Caryl Churchill's *Cloud 9* and the Redefinition of Queer Rhetoric", argues that there are certain characteristics of rhetoric relating to homosexuality and queer behaviors in texts through the centuries, evolving to fit the opinions and beliefs of the culture during the particular time period. However, one notable trend that seems to follow gay/queer rhetoric through the ages is the certain connotations that come with it. Caryl Churchill negates typical techniques of gay/queer rhetoric in her play *Cloud 9*, and in turn, creates new rhetoric that challenges the societal opinions of many in Great Britain during the 1970s. This article discusses queer theory and how it relates to prominent texts from respective time periods, such as the rhetoric found in the bible and the works of Oscar Wilde, to ultimately display how *Cloud 9* thwarts the rhetoric and rhetorical theories seen in prior works, as well as exhibit how Churchill protests the societal beliefs of homosexuality in 1970's Great Britain. This paper examines how gay/queer rhetoric has both changed and evolved through the years, from connotations of heresy and destruction, to hidden and ambiguous, to, as Churchill has contributed in her play *Cloud 9*, boastful, assertive, and natural. Churchill not only combats prior and typical queer rhetoric, but also creates new connotations associated with gay/queer language and behaviors that consequently protest the prejudices still existing in 1970's Great Britain. ①

Sonia Firdaus, in "The Reflection of Modern Women in Caryl Churchill *Top Girls* and Anita Nair's *Ladies Coupe*", argues that Caryl Churchill and Anita Nair, both female authors, have highlighted the issues of modern women in *Top Girls* and *Ladies Coupe* respectively. Regardless of their geographical, cultural, religious, social, economical, and political differences, most of the women share one thing in common and that is "affliction". Almost all the personas of both the stories identify and share their agonies, somehow, in a similar way despite the fact that they live in different periods of history. It is possible that a woman can survive alone without registering in the conventional institution of marriage, even though some aspects of her life remain unfulfilled, empty and unyielding because it is against the law of nature. In *Advice on the Choice of a Mistress*, Benjamin Franklin said, a single man "resembles the odd Half of a Pair of Scissors", so it is not just the need of a woman but the man's as well to have a partner to share life with. Nevertheless, the majority of modern women are willing to accept the companionship of men, but they are not intrigued by the marriage institutions. Therefore, the similarities and dissimilarities in both the narratives will be explored with a special reference to modern women's standpoint. ②

2. Feminism

Victoria Bazin, in "'[Not] Talking 'bout My Generation': Historicizing Feminisms in Caryl Churchill's *Top Girls*", examines the play *Top Girls* by Caryl

---

① DeGeorge S. "'From Bugger to Bragger': Caryl Churchill's *Cloud 9* and the Redefinition of Queer Rhetoric". Pennsylvania Literary Journal, 2017, 9(2):60-69.
② Firdaus S. "The Reflection of Modern Women in Caryl Churchill *Top Girls* and Anita Nair's *Ladies Coupe*". Dialogue, 2011, 6(1):57-67.

Churchill. The play, first shown at the Royal Court in 1982, focuses on the relation between feminism and history. The conflict is between two sisters, Marlene who is ambitious and competitive and Joyce, the exploited socialist who takes care of her sister's child. Sisterhood, as depicted in the play, is presented as a source of conflict and tension instead of being the foundation of unity and solidarity. The play exhibits the effect of social and economic changes on feminism. ①

Neslihan Yilmaz Demirkaya, in "Scapegoating Non-Conforming Identities: Witchcraft Hysteria in Arthur Miller's *The Crucible* and Caryl Churchill's *Vinegar Tom*", argues that when people are faced with different takes on their traditions that they firmly cling to so as to remain being who they purport to be, they are generally inclined to ostracise those who are different. In this sense, ostracising people by discarding them from their community is, metaphorically speaking, the same as leaving the goat in the wilderness as the verses from Leviticus explain the history of scapegoating. Just as the goat story from Leviticus, political and patriarchal power groups blame non-conforming individuals for all the problems in society, and ostracise them as witches only to take the upper hand, and enjoy absolute power. The pattern of punishment proves to be the same, that is, to leave the victim alone in a place away from home, be in the wilderness for a goat, or the loneliness and isolation for an individual. Besides, one of the most used and most efficient ways of scapegoating people, as the evidence shows, is to rekindle the tall-tale of witchcraft. This paper explores how and why witchcraft is deployed as a scapegoating strategy to silence and stigmatise non-conforming individuals on the pretext of maintaining order in society in Arthur Miler's *The Crucible* and Caryl

---

① Bazin V. "'[Not] Talking 'bout My Generation': Historicizing Feminisms in Caryl Churchill's *Top Girls*". Studies in the Literary Imagination, 2006, 39(2):115-134.

Churchill's *Vinegar Tom* respectively. ①

Rebecca Cameron, in "From *Great Women* to *Top Girls*: Pageants of Sisterhood in British Feminist Theater", explores British female solidarity that encompasses national, cultural and class boundaries in the theatrical productions *Top Girls*, by Caryl Churchill, *Pageant of Great Women*, by Cicely Hamilton, and the Women's Coronation Procession of June 17, 1911. The author highlights twentieth-century appropriated pageantry to create a concept of female solidarity akin to the feminism of their period. The result of this exercise is the intertwining of women's history, women's power and martyrdom, and women's solidarity. ②

3. Spacial Study

Siân Adiseshiah, in "Utopian Space in Caryl Churchill's History Plays: *Light Shining in Buckinghamshire* and *Vinegar Tom*", explores the relationship among theater, utopia and space elaborated in the theatrical productions *Light Shining in Buckinghamshire* and *Vinegar Tom* by Caryl Churchill; factor that could influence the function of utopianism as a catalyst to social transformation; inclination of theatrical space to the application of utopian theories; overview of the theatrical productions. ③

---

① Demirkaya N Y. "Scapegoating Non-Conforming Identities: Witchcraft Hysteria in Arthur Miller's *The Crucible* and Caryl Churchill's *Vinegar Tom*". Journal of History, Culture & Art Research, 2015, 4(2):123-135.

② Cameron R. "From *Great Women* to *Top Girls*: Pageants of Sisterhood in British Feminist Theater". Comparative Drama, 2009, 43(2):143-166. Feminist Theater.

③ Adiseshiah S. "Utopian Space in Caryl Churchill's History Plays: *Light Shining in Buckinghamshire* and *Vinegar Tom*". Utopian Studies, 2005, 16(1):3-26.

4. New Historicism

Sanja Bahun-Radunović, in "History in Postmodern Theater: Heiner Müller, Caryl Churchill, and Suzan-Lori Parks", focuses on "the reassessments of history in postmodern theater address what is also the crucial tension-point in contemporary philosophy of history and historiography". According to the author, postmodern theater approaches the revision of the concept of history through the questioning of teleological stories. In connection, the experimental strategies most often deployed include the intertextual inclusion of archival and quasi-archival material. [1]

Brean S. Hammond, in "'Is Everything History?': Churchill, Barker, and the Modern History Play", examines the early works of two writers, Caryl Churchill and Howard Barker. Churchill's early work with the Joint Stock Company considers the nature of socialism and the degree of its compatibility with feminism. Two plays that form part of the early repertoire of the Joint Stock Company are compared. [2]

---

[1] Bahun-Radunović S. "History in Postmodern Theater: Heiner Müller, Caryl Churchill, and Suzan-Lori Parks". Comparative Literature Studies, 2008, 45(4):446-470.

[2] Hammond B S. "'Is Everything History?': Churchill, Barker, and the Modern History Play". Comparative Drama, 2007, 41(1):1-23.

Part II American Dramatists

Chapter 10

Eugene O'Neill

Eugene O'Neill (1888-1953)

O'Neill was an epoch-making playwright in the history of American drama. He created a sense of unease in the literary and dramatic circles. His work constituted American's claim and created a powerful modern dramatic literature. His best known works include *Beyond the Horizon*, *The Emperor Jones*, *Desire Under the Elms*, *The Iceman Cometh*, and *Long Day's Journey Into Night*. He won the Nobel Prize in Literature in 1936.

Critical Perspectives

1. Biographical Study

Alexander Pettit, in "The Texts of Eugene O'Neill's *The Fountain*: Indigeneity, Stereotype, Survivance", offers information on journalist Elizabeth Shepley Sergeant who recalls Eugene O'Neill, playwright with sympathy for the Indians from childhood. In his play *The Fountain*, the Indians remove white men. It focuses on O'Neill's indigenes as passive receptors of disgraceful ideology.[①]

2. Thematic Study

Mojtaba Jeihouni, and Nasser Maleki, in "Far from the Madding Civilization: Anarcho-primitivism and Revolt against Disintegration in Eugene O'Neill's *The Hairy Ape*", argues that "Anarcho-primitivism contends that modern civilization deprives people of their happiness, which is why it seeks to reconstruct civilization on a primitive basis, one that holds concrete promises of happiness. It argues that a harmonious relation with human nature and external nature needs to be established by translating technological societies into societies that are free of hierarchy, domination, class relationships, and, simply put, of modern structures. Anarcho-primitivists intend to reinstate a primitive outlook in the modern era and recover the

---

① Pettit A. "The Texts of Eugene O'Neill's *The Fountain*: Indigeneity, Stereotype, Survivance". Texas Studies in Literature & Language, 2019, 61(2):193-223.

authenticity and wholeness lost to the tyranny of civilization. The radical nature of Yank's anti-authoritarianism in Eugene O'Neill's *The Hairy Ape* (1921) demonstrates that he is totally at a loss about the positive functions of industrialism. We argue that Yank expresses a deep resentment toward civilization that is barely hidden in the play. This leads us to suggest that Yank's objective is not dissimilar from that of anarcho-primitivists: he values his individuality and tries to subvert the social forces that are arrayed against it. Like anarcho-primitivists, he is determined to bring down the pillars of the material culture in favor of a primitive life, where free subjectivity or individuation becomes the integral gift of society."[1]

Banu Öğünç, in "Where Do I Belong? Power and Class Struggle in *Miss Julie* and *The Hairy Ape*", argues that written in 1888 by Swedish playwright August Strindberg, *Miss Julie* is considered as a naturalistic play that deals with power struggles between the characters Jean and Julie in terms of gender and class. As an over-reacher, Jean tries to overpower Julie in order to upgrade his social position. *The Hairy Ape*, on the other hand, is an expressionistic play which was written by American playwright Eugene O'Neill in 1922. The play is about the degraded position of Yank who searches for his social place in the society. After being labeled as a "filthy beast" by the daughter of a steel company owner, Yank internalizes his status as an ape like creature. Throughout the play, he involves in a quest as he tries to belong to a social class. Although written in two different centuries reflecting different cultures and cultural problems, both plays employ male characters who struggle to improve their position within the hierarchal and material society in spite of the status quo they face. Their struggle also includes the male characters' questioning of power over female characters. Consequently, this article aims to

---

[1] Jeihouni M, Maleki N. "Far from the Madding Civilization: Anarcho-primitivism and Revolt against Disintegration in Eugene O'Neill's *The Hairy Ape*". International Journal of English Studies, 2016, 16(2):61-80.

analyze *Miss Julie* and *The Hairy Ape* in order to illustrate power struggles of the male characters that transgress one century to century and one culture to another preserving the core of the problems of the class issue in the modern society. ①

3. Psychological Study

Martin Weegmann, in "Eugene O'Neill's Hughie and the Grandiose Addict", offers a view on the role of grandiosity in addicted individuals—its self-protective and self-sustaining functions. Starting with a discussion of a fictional gambler, as described in a play by Eugene O'Neill, it continues with a discussion of the dynamic of aggrandizement, drawing on theoretical literature. ②

Maria T. Miliora, in "Heinz Kohut and Eugene O'Neill: An Essay on the Application of Self Psychology to O'Neill's Dramas", examines the relation between the dramatizations of playwright Eugene O'Neill and the thinking of psychoanalyst Heinz Kohut; background of Kohut and O'Neill; discussion of early psychoanalytic literature on O'Neill; methodology of applied self-psychological studies of literature. ③

Christer Sjödin, in "Obstacles to Development—Reflections on Eugene O'Neill's Play *A Moon for the Misbegotten*. Special Reference to Banter, Fear and Suspicion", discussed Eugene O'Neill's play *A Moon for the Misbegotten* with special reference to banter, fear and suspicion. The dead mother is used to

---

① Öğünç B. "Where Do I Belong? Power and Class Struggle in *Miss Julie* and *The Hairy Ape*". Gaziantep University Journal of Social Sciences, 2018, 17(3):857-865.

② Weegmann M. "Eugene O'Neill's Hughie and the Grandiose Addict". Psychodynamic Practice, 2002, 8(1):21-32.

③ Miliora M T. "Heinz Kohut and Eugene O'Neill: An Essay on the Application of Self Psychology to O'Neill's Dramas". Annual of Psychoanalysis, 2000(28): 245-259.

understand the characters as well as the oedipal situation and the fear of the stranger. ①

Martin Weegmann, in "'We're All Poor Nuts and Things Happen, and We Just Get Mixed in Wrong, That's All' Lessons for Psychotherapy from Eugene O'Neill's Play, *Anna Christie*", argues that *Anna Christie*, by the Irish American playwright Eugene O'Neill, is a powerful play, depicting hurt emotions, injured selves and the hardened exteriors that people fashion to blame and afford a measure of protection. It relays the story of an abandoned daughter and her reunion with her father, their (relative) reconciliation, and meeting a new man, and the consequences of her revelation of prostitution. From textual analysis of the play, the paper explores themes of shame, repudiation and self-protection, including the formidable, or ultimate defence of "unassailability". It is argued that the psychotherapist has something valuable to learn from this harrowing and evocative work of literature. ②

Jesse Weiner, in "O'Neill's Aeneid: Virgilian Allusion in *Mourning Becomes Electra*", traces "a system of allusion to Virgil's *Aeneid* in Eugene O'Neill's adaptation of the *Oresteia*, *Mourning Becomes Electra*. O'Neill's drunken and enigmatic sailor has no corresponding character in Aeschylus' *Oresteia*, nor in its subsequent classical iterations. As I show, the Chantyman is explicitly crafted after the mythological Charon, imported from Book 6 of Virgil's *Aeneid*. Moreover, the use of this epic archetype serves to promote O'Neill's mechanism of predetermined causality, both by means of its thematic implications and structural position within

---

① Sjödin C. "Obstacles to Development—Reflections on Eugene O'Neill's Play *A Moon for the Misbegotten*. Special Reference to Banter, Fear and Suspicion". International Forum of Psychoanalysis, 2003, 12(4):206-212.

② Weegmann M. "'We're All Poor Nuts and Things Happen, and We Just Get Mixed in Wrong, That's All' Lessons for Psychotherapy from Eugene O'Neill's Play, *Anna Christie*". Psychodynamic Practice, 2016, 22(2):131-141.

the narrative of *Aeneid* 6. The allusion recalls the Virgilian unveiling of Aeneas' familial destiny and thereby underscores the broader and inevitable consequences of Brant's death upon the House of Mannon. Ultimately, this intertextual strategy augments O'Neill's self-professed project in this play: to recreate on the modern stage a tragic world order governed by fate, in the conspicuous absence of a divine apparatus."①

Thomas Connors, in "Extreme O'Neill", presents an examination into the plays of American dramatist Eugene O'Neill. Details are given to describe the writer's distinct use of language, and subtext and specific stage directions and comments are offered by several directors regarding different ways to interpret and re-stage his work. Discussion is particularly offered to question the level of experimentalism which can be applied to the texts.②

Richard Hornby, in "Inner Conflict", focuses on the depiction of inner conflict in several dramas written by Eugene O'Neill, the son of the great stage actor James O'Neill. Inner conflict is considered as the soul of O'Neill's great drama. Inner conflict in drama involves the use of wordy dialogues, obvious characterization and awkward plots. One of his plays that utilized the concept was *A Touch of The Poet*.③

4. New Historicism

Jeffrey Ullom, in "Fear Mongering, Media Intimidation, and Political Machinations: Tracing the Agendas behind the *All God's Chillun Got Wings*

---

① Weiner J. "O'Neill's Aeneid: Virgilian Allusion in *Mourning Becomes Electra*". International Journal of the Classical Tradition, 2013, 20(1/2):41-60.
② Connors T. "Extreme O'Neill". American Theatre, 2009, 26(2):22-25.
③ Hornby R. "Inner Conflict". Hudson Review, 2006, 59(1):107-114.

Controversy", stresses the need for re-examining Eugene O'Neill's *All God's Chillun Got Wings*, in terms of political agendas. Described as a case of racial tolerance, the drama also involves personal threats, government action and constant attacks from the press mounted by two political powers. Several works that have provided insights on O'Neill's drama included *Staging O'Neill: The Experimental Years, 1920-1934*, by Ronald H. Wainscott and *Tempest in Black and White: The 1924 Premiere of Eugene O'Neill's "All God's Chillun Got Wings"*, by Glenda Frank. ①

Kevin Spinale, in "O'Neill's Dark Passage", discusses criticisms of playwright Eugene O'Neill's plays. According to the author, the periodical's critics are harsh on O'Neill. While O'Neill's plays are successful and innovative, they depict acts of murder, violence and social evils. Some of his plays are *Mourning Becomes Electra*, *Strange Interlude*, and *A Long Day's Journey Into Night*. Elizabeth Jordan, one of the critics, depicts O'Neill's world as sinister and sunless. ②

Margaret E. Styles and Theresa G. Coble, in "Local Legacies: Factors Influencing the Relationship between Literary Sites and Local Communities", argues that protected historic sites are often in close proximity to, or surrounded by, a community. The relationship between an historic site and its local community may affect the significance and meanings ascribed to the site, as well as the level of site promotion and visitation. "The purpose of this qualitative study was to (1) determine what factors influence the degree of support communities provide to local historic sites, specifically literary sites, and (2) provide site managers with a conceptual framework that can be used to build stronger relationships with their

---

① Ullom J. "Fear Mongering, Media Intimidation, and Political Machinations: Tracing the Agendas behind the *All God's Chillun Got Wings* Controversy". Comparative Drama, 2011, 45(2):81-97.

② Spinale K. "O'Neill's Dark Passage". America, 2013, 209(16):22-23.

communities." There were two phases to this research project. The first phase uses phone interviews to explore the potential factors that may influence site-community relations for 17 U. S. literary sites. The second phase focuses on a specific literary site, Eugene O'Neill National Historic Site (NHS) in Danville, California. Interviews are conducted to explore the meanings, significance, and degree of place attachment Danville community members ascribe to the O'Neill historic site. Five factors emerge from the literary site interviews: centrality of the site, community's sense of identity with the writer, writer's connection to their community, literary site outreach programming, and community partnerships. The factors incorporate potential positive and negative effects to the literary site-community relations. Study results suggest that the O'Neill historic site in Danville has a low relative score of influential factors, contributing to a low level of place attachment among the community members. Other sites, such as William Faulkner's Rowan Oak in Oxford, Mississippi, have a high relative score of influential factors leading to a strong literary site-community connection. The conceptual framework developed from the study illustrates the correlation between the key constructs from existing literature, the literary site influential factors, and site-community specific issues. When the Danville community focus group results are applied to the framework, it indicates that there is a higher level of negative rather than positive influences on the Danville-O'Neill site relationship. The findings are significant and influence the stewardship ethic or preservation efforts of the community towards the site. Managers can apply the conceptual framework at their literary and historic sites to assess the extent to which the identified factors are positively or negatively influencing local site-community relations. Identifying these factors and their influences may assist site managers in determining where to focus efforts to develop more effective community outreach programs and build stronger relationships with their local communities. ①

5. Performing Art

Russell M. Dembin, in "Literary Manager: Lexy Leuszler", profiles Lexy Leuszler, literary manager of the Eugene O'Neill Theater Center in Waterford, Connecticut, and argues that she is responsible for managing 2,500-plus submissions from aspiring applicants and artists and representing the O'Neill's mission and values. She is committed to making theatre more inclusive. ②

6. Canonization Study

Terry Teachout, in "America's Greatest Playwright?", discusses critical responses to the work of American playwright Eugene O'Neill in the 20th and 21st centuries. The author emphasizes positive reception of works published during his lifetime including *Ah, Wilderness!*, *The Emperor Jones*, and *Anna Christie* and compares these plays to O'Neill's posthumous plays, including *Long Day's Journey*, *A Moon for the Misbegotten*, and *A Touch of the Poet*. Topics include poetics, simplicity, and characters in the plays. ③

---

① Styles M E, Coble T G. "Local Legacies: Factors Influencing the Relationship between Literary Sites and Local Communities". Journal of Park & Recreation Administration, 2007, 25(3):89-112.
② Dembin R M. "Literary Manger: Lexy Leuszler". American Theatre, 2018, 35(10):27.
③ Teachout T. "America's Greatest Playwright?". Commentary, 2011, 131(3):75-78.

7. Cultural Study

Carme Manuel, in "A Ghost in the Expressionist Jungle of O'Neill's *The Emperor Jones*", presents the idea of examining the treatment of the African American on the American stage by Eugene O'Neill in his play *The Emperor Jones*; role of the play in bringing Provincetown players their first recognition from Broadway audiences and managers; consideration of the play as the first American play to cast black actors; positive reviews of the play by white critics; artistic representations of the truth of Negro life; O'Neill's ways of racial representation in drama. [1]

Pamela S. Saur, in "Classifying Rural Dramas: O'Neill's *Desire under the Elms* and Schönherr's *Erde*", presents information on two of the plays, *Desire under the Elms* by Eugene O'Neill and *Erde* by Karl Schönherr. It can be used to demonstrate how literary works that are similar in content may be evaluated differently depending upon differing cultural, literary, and historical contexts. O'Neill's play highlights the rivalry between a 75-year-old New England farmer, Ephraim Cabot, and his middle-aged son. Schönherr's 1909 play, *Erde*, revolves around a 76-year-old patriarchal farm tyrant. Both plays are "rural" not only because of their setting, but because this rural setting is mandatory to them. Owning and cultivating rural land forms an integral issue in both plays. The relationship to the land is the determining factor in the familial and sex roles, as well as the self-concepts and the relative status of the characters, and the essential conflicts of the two dramas. In both plays, the traditional ideals of both manhood and womanhood are discussed primarily in terms of control over farm property and its operation, with

---

[1] Manuel C. "A Ghost in the Expressionist Jungle of O'Neill's *The Emperor Jones*". African American Review, 2005, 39(1/2):67-85.

the desire to be fertile and propagate.①

John Patrick Diggins, in "Eugene O'Neill's America", presents a discussion of playwright Eugene O'Neill's work as a source for U.S. higher education courses in the classics, philosophy, history, political science, and gender studies, adapted from the book *Eugene O'Neill's America: Desire under Democracy* by John Patrick Diggins.②

8. Gender Study

Mark Masterson, in "'It's Queer, It's Like Fate': Tracking Queer in O'Neill's *Mourning Becomes Electra*", presents a case study of *Mourning Becomes Electra*, a trilogy written by Eugene O'Neill as a modern performance of classical plays, Oresteia and Oedipus Rex. It focuses on how and why the word "queer" occurs 31 times in the trilogy. It discusses the various meanings that attached to the word within the context of the play, and how its repeated presence is generally in reference to manhood that is turned in on itself.③

Tara Harney-Mahajan, in "Refashioning the Wedding Dress as the 'Future Anterior' in Marina Carr and Edna O'Brien", discusses the wedding dress, a representation of weddings and sociology. Topics discussed include women's studies, literary studies and anthropology. Plays including *Long Day's Journey into Night* by Eugene O'Neill, *By the Bog of Cats* by Marina Carr and *Haunted* by Edna O'Brien are also discussed.④

---

① Saur P S. "Classifying Rural Dramas: O'Neill's *Desire under the Elms* and Schönherr's *Erde*". Modern Austrian Literature, 1993, 26(3/4):101-114.

② Diggins J P. "Eugene O'Neill's America". Chronicle of Higher Education, 2007, 53(35):14-15.

③ Masterson M. "'It's Queer, It's Like Fate': Tracking Queer in O'Neill's *Mourning Becomes Electra*". Helios, 2011, 38(2):131-147.

④ Harney-Mahajan T. "Refashioning the Wedding Dress as the 'Future Anterior' in Marina Carr and Edna O'Brien". Women's Studies, 2015, 44(7):996-1021.

Chapter 11

Arthur Miller

Arthur Miller (1915-2005)

Miller was one of America's most famous playwrights of the twentieth century. Miller wrote plays on broad social themes. He put a special emphasis on depicting the inner thoughts of individuals and their conflicts with the morality of their society. His major works include *All My Sons*, *Death of a Salesman*, in which Miller has been pulled, again and again, back to that traumatic decade, even in the 1960s and 1970s.

Critical Perspectives

1. Biographical Study

Sarah Churchwell, in "Requiem for an American Dream", considers themes of the American dream in the works of playwright Arthur Miller, including his plays *The American Clock*, *Death of a Salesman*, *After the Fall*, as well as his autobiography, *Timebends: A Life*. Topics include faith in rags-to-riches narratives, materialism, selfishness, and redemption. Biographical details include the impact of the Great Depression on Miller's family, his marriage to the actress Marilyn Monroe, and his response to being called by the House Committee on Un-American Activities.①

Leo Robson, in "They Might Be Giants", looks at the lives and careers of American playwright Arthur Miller and American novelist Saul Bellow, focusing on the critical reception each received at different points in their career. It discusses works by them including Miller's play *Death of a Salesman* and Bellow's novel *The Adventures of Augie March*.②

James Lardner, in "A Miller's Tale", focuses on the book *Timebends: A Life*, by Arthur Miller. Miller is not what the author would call a representative man of the times, and yet of all the writers of his generation who have given their autobiographies. The author knows of none who has so persuasively captured the political journey from the 1930s to the 1950s and beyond—or who has done a better

---

① Churchwell S. "Requiem for an American Dream". New Statesman, 2019, 148(5460):46-50.
② Robson L. "They Might Be Giants". New Statesman, 2015, 144(5260):52-57.

job of explaining why the early revelation of Marxism's promise took hold so swiftly and completely, why the later revelation of Marxism's actuality was so stubbornly resisted and how both revelations shaped art and life. ①

Robert Sylvester, in "Brooklyn Boy Makes Good", narrates the life story of Arthur Miller, author of the Broadway hit *Death of a Salesman* in Brooklyn, New York. He was called the most capable playwright and his play became the biggest box-office blast. He is usually accepted as a reliable and most capable writer of stage tragedies since Eugene O'Neill. His work was criticized by most critics as the spectacular dramatic success in the theatrical history. ②

2. Thematic Study

Khondakar Md. Hadiuzzaman and Md. Zahedul Kabir, in "Unveiling the Glamour of Salesmanship in Arthur Miller's *Death of a Salesman*", argues that salesmanship is a dynamic element of marketing strategy where selling plays a vital role in an industrial economy. As a profession, salesmanship is glamorous in capitalistic economy as it promotes sales of goods and services worth billions and billions of dollars. Moreover, it offers handsome salaries and bright prospects that persuade an ordinary salesman to rise to the top executive position. But salesmanship is not only lucrative but also illusory and exploiting. Arthur Miller's *Death of a Salesman* deals with the theme of salesmanship and focuses on the dark side of this profession through his dramatic lens. This paper attempts to show how Miller unveils the glamour of salesmanship through his tragic protagonist Willy Loman, and proves that this capitalistic aspect can cause frustration and leads an

---

① Lardner J. "A Miller's Tale". Nation, 1987, 245(18):632-636.
② Sylvester R. "Brooklyn Boy Makes Good". Saturday Evening Post, 1949, 222(3):26-100.

employee to ruin.①

Bert Cardullo, in "*Death of a Salesman*, Life of a Jew: Ethnicity, Business, and the Character of Willy Loman", presents literary criticism of the play *Death of a Salesman* by Arthur Miller. It focuses on the character of Willy Loman and presents an overview of the play's major themes. The author discusses the accuracy of ethnicity as presented in the play by focusing on Miller's use of language. The question is raised of whether the representation of American business practices in the play is a true theme or a superficial explanation for Willy Loman's troubles.②

3. New Historicism

Terry W. Thompson, in "'All I Want Is Out There': The Wild West Subtext in Arthur Miller's *Death of a Salesman*", examines the subtext of the play regarding the American West, suggesting that the opportunity and redemption associated with the region is reflected in the characters of the Loman family. Particular attention is given to how urban settings are portrayed in the play.③

4. Narratology Study

Terry W. Thompson, in "'Built Like Adonises'": Evoking Greek Icons in *Death of a Salesman*", examines the Greek mythological icons that evoke in the character Willy Loman, who believes that her two sons are destined for success in

---

① Hadiuzzaman K M, Kabir M Z. "Unveiling the Glamour of Salesmanship in Arthur Miller's *Death of a Salesman*". ASA University Review, 2018, 12(2):71-78.

② Cardullo B. "*Death of a Salesman*, Life of a Jew: Ethnicity, Business, and the Character of Willy Loman". Southwest Review, 2007, 92(4):583-596.

③ Thompson T W. "'All I Want Is Out There': The Wild West Subtext in Arthur Miller's *Death of a Salesman*". Midwest Quarterly, 2018, 59(3):331-342.

their endeavors because of their good looks and charisma. It also looks at Loman's comparison of her two sons with Greek icons Adonis and Hercules, who were only famed for their good looks and strong muscles. [1]

5. Psychological Study

Daniel Thomières, in "All Is Not Gold: Fatherhood and Identity in Arthur Miller's *Death of a Salesman*", tries to "shed some light on Arthur Miller's *Death of a Salesman*. It starts with an analysis of a seemingly irrelevant detail: the difference between gold and diamonds. Gold must be seen as a symptom pointing to Willy Loman's obsession for imitation, which can be accounted for by a specific form of pathological narcissism, itself caused by a faulty representation of the structure of fatherhood in his unconscious. From there, it will prove necessary to question the protagonist's peculiar relation to naming, especially his use of the Name of the Father. The approach chosen will be interpretative systematically progressing from symptoms to structures that are both ever more abstract and specific. In other words, the problem raised is to determine how far one can go from a theoretical point of view in order to reconstruct the logic governing Willy's unconscious." [2]

6. Cultural Study

Lee Siegel, in "Willy Loman's Secret", presents a critical analysis of the play

---

[1] Thompson T W. "'Built Like Adonises': Evoking Greek Icons in *Death of a Salesman*". Midwest Quarterly, 2016, 57(3):276-287.

[2] Thomières D. "All Is Not Gold: Fatherhood and Identity in Arthur Miller's *Death of a Salesman*". PsyArt, 2016(20):1-23.

Death of a Salesman by Arthur Miller. It discusses the failures of the protagonist, Willy Loman, in relation to a capitalist economic system. It profiles the other characters and analyzes their family relationships. Also mentioned is the history of revivals of the play.[①]

Rui Pina Coelho, in "Be Violent Again: Violence, Realism and Consumerism in Arthur Miller's *Death of A Salesman* and Mark Ravenhill's *Shopping and Fucking*", argues that the 1950s is a seminal period for the configuration of violence in modern drama and a crucial moment for the fusion between violence and realism. "In post-war drama, we will not see violence portrayed as an extreme action or as unbelievable acts. Violence becomes the natural way to express social and individual tensions, through class conflicts, strong language and war motives. Themes such as the display of physical violence, the failure of the human body, exposing dysfunctional families and war effects, becomes more and more common and attached to everyday life. This was fertile ground for John Osborne, Edward Bond or Arthur Miller, or for the British dramaturgy of the nineties, especially with the so-called in-yer-face theatre. Thus, I will focus on the effects this discussion had on Portuguese culture and theatre. I will discuss two performances that are both representative of the Portuguese alternative culture of the time and that stage texts that deal with realistic violence: Arthur Miller's *Death of a Salesman* by Experimental Theatre of Oporto (TEP), in 1954; and Mark Ravenhill's *Shopping and Fucking*, directed by Gonçalo Amorim, in 2007. Both performances represent straightforward approaches to the texts and raise several interesting aspects: how is violence portrayed in Portugal, in 1954, when a fascist dictatorship imposed a severe censorship on performances? And how is Ravenhill's violence replaced by

---

① Siegel L. "Willy Loman's Secret". The Nation, 2012, 294(18):28-30.

irony in the performance by Gonçalo Amorim?"[1]

7. Artistic Study

Mike Pepi, in "Critical Winter", offers information related to the impact of artificial intelligence on the art industry. It mentions about involvement of AI in art mentioned in the book *The Artist in the Machine: The World of AI-Powered Creativity* by Arthur Miller; and thousands of portrait photos to create images of people who never existed mentioned in the book *Portraits of Imaginary People* by Michael Tyka.[2]

---

[1] Coelho R P. "Be Violent Again: Violence, Realism and Consumerism in Arthur Miller's *Death of a Salesman* and Mark Ravenhill's *Shopping and Fucking*". Cartaphilus, 2016(14):363-375.

[2] Pepi M. "Critical Winter". Art in America, 2020, 108(4):26-29.

Chapter 12

Tennessee Williams

Tennessee Williams(1911-1983)

Tennessee Williams has certainly become one of the greatest American dramatists to go down in the country's literary history. Now universally accepted as one of America's classic playwrights, he is in evidence practically everywhere in the theaters of the nation. Williams are thematically rather sensational. His works include *The Glass Menagerie* and *Suddenly Last Summer*.

Critical Perspectives

1. Biographical Study

John S. Bak, in "'Love to You and Mother': An Unpublished Letter of Tennessee Williams to His Father, Cornelius Coffin Williams, 1945", discusses a letter written by American playwright Tennessee Williams to his father, Cornelius Coffin Williams, dated January 14, 1945. Topics discussed include Williams' relationship with his father, the writing of the letter at the Sherman Hotel in Chicago, Illinois during the tryouts of his play *The Glass Menagerie*, and rising interest in his other play *You Touched Me!*. [1]

Mark Cave, in "Something Wild in the Country: The Fugitive Life of Tennessee Williams", discusses the early years and career of U. S. playwright Tennessee Williams. The author examines the development of Williams' literary talent. His education in a journalism program at the University of Missouri in Columbia and, later, at the University of Iowa is detailed. The production, and subsequent failure, of his play *Battle of Angels* is explained, as well as his often tenuous financial situation in early life. The relationship he developed with literary agent Audrey Wood is discussed. [2]

Joyce Durham, in "Portrait of a Friendship: Selected Correspondence between

---

[1] Bak J S. "'Love to You and Mother': An Unpublished Letter of Tennessee Williams to His Father, Cornelius Coffin Williams, 1945". Mississippi Quarterly, 2016, 69(3):347-352.

[2] Cave M. "Something Wild in the Country: The Fugitive Life of Tennessee Williams". Southern Quarterly, 2011, 48(4):11-31.

Carson McCullers and Tennessee Williams", examines the correspondence exchanged between novelist Carson McCullers and playwright Tennessee Williams. The letters, an archive of correspondence between the two writers maintained by Duke University, shed light on the friendship and the work habits of Williams and McCullers. Letters addressing the work of contemporary writers, such as Gore Vidal and Arthur Miller, are also contained in the article. ①

Julia M. Klein, in "Strange History", critiques the book *Tennessee Williams: Mad Pilgrimage of the Flesh* by John Lahr, focusing on several of Williams' plays including *In the Bar of a Tokyo Hotel*, *The Glass Menagerie*, and *A Streetcar Named Desire*. Autobiographical plays are addressed, along with various literary themes such as beauty, grief, and the efforts to redeem life. Theater producer Lyle Leverich's book *Tom: The Unknown Tennessee Williams* is mentioned, along with Williams' private life. ②

Nicholas R. Moschovakis, in "Tennessee Williams and the Ambivalence of Success", presents a critical analysis of Tennessee Williams's life and literary career, including poetic plays written by Williams, obsession of Williams with oppressed circumstances of Van Gogh's life, disillusionment of Williams with money and fame, association of Williams's fictional heroines with genteel decadence, theme of the play *Not About Nightingales*, and portrayal of fantasy in the play *Stairs to the Roof*. ③

C. Allen Haake, in "Exorcizing Blue Devils: *The Night of the Iguana* as Tennessee Williams's Ultimate Confessional", focuses on the publication of *The Night of the Iguana*, by Tennessee Williams. When *The Night of the Iguana* was

---

① Durham J. "Portrait of a Friendship: Selected Correspondence between Carson McCullers and Tennessee Williams". Mississippi Quarterly, Winter 2005/Spring 2006, 59(1/2):5-16.

② Klein J M. "Strange History". The Nation, 2014, 299(20):40-42.

③ Moschovakis N R. "Tennessee Williams and the Ambivalence of Success". Sewanee Review, 2002, 110(3):483-490.

published in 1961, Williams had found comparative stability in his life. It was the first time that Williams understood his emotional dependency on his sister named Rose. Rose was his tie to the sweetness and warmth of his childhood which had vanished long age.①

Lonnie Firestone, in "Not Just About Nightingales", profiles American playwright Tennessee Williams. It offers information on his struggles in the mid-1930s before he attracted the interest of Willard Hollard, director of the Mummers theater company. It examines the political and social issues explored by Williams in *Candles to the Sun* and his motivation to write *Not About Nightingales*. It discusses his entry into Broadway with a grant from the Rockefeller Foundation and the continued use of desperate characters in his plays.②

2. Psychoanalytical Study

Leila Rezaei Hezaveh, Nurul Farhana Low Bt Abdullah, and Md Salleh Yaapar, in "Reconstructing an Identity: A Psychoanalytical Reading of *The Night of the Iguana* by Tennessee Williams", attempts to "detect Tennessee Williams's psychological development in his last successful play *The Night of the Iguana* (1961) in comparison with his previous plays which pronounced his fragmented identity. A comparison between Tennessee Williams's *Suddenly Last Summer* (1958) and *The Night of the Iguana* detects a sudden shift of the dramatist's mind in the application of symbols and images employed. A psychoanalytical assessment and comparison of symbols, images and literary devices applied in both plays will depict the dramatist's constitution of his tenuous 'I' and reconstruction of his

---

① Haake C A. "Exorcizing Blue Devils: *The Night of the Iguana* as Tennessee Williams's Ultimate Confessional". Mississippi Quarterly, Winter 2004/Spring 2005, 58(1/2):105-118.

② Firestone L. "Not Just about Nightingales". American Theatre, 2011, 28(7):32-33.

distorted identity. Unlike the horrifying images of God, cannibalism and melancholia resulting from abjection that imposed a certain Gothic atmosphere in *Suddenly Last Summer*, the images and settings in *The Night of the Iguana* resonate with comfort and leisure which resemble the pre-symbolic." The study therefore suggests that Williams's abundant use of natural symbols and images, particularly the God image in *The Night of the Iguana* presents the setting as the chora which Kristeva defines as the place where the infant's identity is merged with his/her mother before gaining an identity after the mirror stage and the learning of language which marks subsequent entry into the symbolic order. "This analysis therefore helps to bring some clarity to the play, particularly in the light of prior criticism levelled against Williams for his excessive use of symbols and natural images." ①

Daniel Thomières, in "Tennessee Williams and the Two Streetcars", analyzes the play *A Streetcar Named Desire* by Tennessee Williams, focusing on its portrayal of desire and its disordered relationships with love, sexuality, and mourning. The philosophical differences between desire and need are discussed along with illustrations of their thematic representations within the play. ②

Janice Siegel, in "Tennessee Williams' *Suddenly Last Summer* and Euripides' *Bacchae*", argues that "Tennessee Williams' 1958 play (and subsequent film) *Suddenly Last Summer* resonates strongly with many of the themes and plot details of Euripides' *Bacchae*. Much of the action in both plays turns on the consequences of a perverse sexuality born of repression (manifested among other ways as a disturbing sexual connection between mother and son)." Other shared themes include the son's search for a god he sees as a destroyer, the irresistible pull of eros, the

---

① Hezaveh L R, Bt Abdullah N F, Yaapar M S. "Reconstructing an Identity: A Psychoanalytical Reading of *The Night of the Iguana* by Tennessee Williams". International Journal of Applied Psychoanalytic Studies, 2015(12):325-335.

② Thomières D. "Tennessee Williams and the Two Streetcars". Midwest Quarterly, 2012, 53(4): 374-391.

consequences of the psychological fragmentation of an individual, the struggle between those who seek to reveal truth and those who are determined to conceal it, and the participation of a mother in the destruction of her own child. "Each male protagonist is pursued, ripped apart, and consumed by the members of a community he sexually infiltrated." The truth about each sparagmos (rending) and omophagia (raw-eating) is uncovered in similar scenes between "psychotherapist" and amnesia victim. But while the truth brings destruction to each murdered man's mother, only in *Suddenly Last Summer* is anyone saved by the awful revelation.①

Laura Michiels and Christophe Collard, in "Double Exposures: On the Reciprocity of Influence between Tennessee Williams and Jean Cocteau", presents an analysis of the principle of reciprocity of influence represented in the works of playwrights Tennessee Williams and Jean Cocteau. It discusses an argument which demonstrates the mutual influence of both playwrights based on hybrid artistry as prime mover and reciprocity as connecting agent to highlight the structural relations of the production context. It also describes the shared fascination of the two playwrights with the Orpheus myth.②

W. Scott Griffies, in "*A Streetcar Named Desire* and Tennessee Williams' Object-relational Conflicts", argues that "Art, as a symbolic expression, often reflects intrapsychic conflicts within the artist, and many of Tennessee Williams' plays contain themes of desperate loneliness, human disconnectedness, and victimization between the powerful and the weak. Williams' genius as a playwright did not save him from painful depression that contained the above themes. He described his internal conflict as a psychic split between identifications with his aggressive, alcoholic father and his sensitive, artistic Dakin (that is, maternal)

---

① Siegel J. "Tennessee Williams' *Suddenly Last Summer* and Euripides' *Bacchae*". International Journal of the Classical Tradition, 2005, 11(4):538-570.

② Michiels L, Collard C. "Double Exposures: On the Reciprocity of Influence between Tennessee Williams and Jean Cocteau". Comparative Drama, 2013, 47(4):505-527.

roots. Of his plays *A Streetcar Named Desire* is one of the most compelling. This paper examines the Blanche/Stanley victim/victimizer paradigm as the dramatization of a core conflict within Williams. Using historical data from his biographies, the author attempts to explicate the hypothesis that in Williams a 'Stanley' representation was in violent conflict with a 'Blanche' representation. The author proposes that this conflict significantly shaped Williams' psychic organization and became a central and oft-repeated theme in his art and his life."[1]

3. New Historicism

Philip C. Kolin, in "'Darling' Pru: Four Unpublished Tennessee Williams Letters to Truman Capote", attempts to detect "Archived at the Historic New Orleans Collection are four unpublished Tennessee Williams's letters, written from Rome and Paris in the late 1940s and early 1950s, to an unidentified recipient named Pru. This article includes these four letters, with the permission of the Williams Estate, and argues that Pru is actually Truman Capote (an example of Williams camping a name) based upon the people, places, times, and events mentioned in the letters. Valuable literary artifacts, these letters shed light on the circle of gay expatriate writers to which Williams and Capote belonged and give us a window into the complicated relationship Williams had with Capote. In the course of his correspondence to Pru, Williams reveals his fears about casting for the film adaptations of *The Rose Tattoo* and *Orpheus Descending*, including his candid opinions of Anna Magnani, James Dean, Marlon Brando, and others."[2]

---

[1] Griffies W S. "*A Streetcar Named Desire* and Tennessee Williams' Object-relational Conflicts". International Journal of Applied Psychoanalytic Studies, 2007, 4(2):110-127.

[2] Kolin P C. "'Darling' Pru: Four Unpublished Tennessee Williams Letters to Truman Capote". Journal of Modern Literature, 2014, 37(2):161-176.

Joanna Kurowska, in "Colonialism in the French Quarter: Tennessee Williams and Joseph Conrad", explores the possible influence of author Joseph Conrad on author Tennessee Williams. Emphasis is given to similarities between Conrad's novella *Heart of Darkness* and Williams' play *A Streetcar Named Desire*. The author also considers problems of race, gender, and history in the works of both authors. Other topics include portrayals of indigenous people, the literary use of symbolic music, and colonialism.[①]

Robert Rea, in "Tennessee Williams's *The Rose Tattoo*: Sicilian Migration and the Mississippi Gulf Coast", discusses a group of Sicilian immigrants living on the Mississippi Gulf Coast featured in the play, the grounded globalism of Williams's Gulf Coast, the failure of scholars to find a historical precedent for Sicilian migration to the Mississippi Gulf Coast and the diverse representation of the South than standardized narratives of southern literature.[②]

Brenda Murphy, in "Toward a Map for the Camino Real: Tennessee Williams's Cultural Imaginary", examines the role of imagination and the imaginative process in the artistic creation of the play, and focuses on the influence of cultural imagery. Williams' allusions to the book *Don Quixote* by Miguel de Cervantes, and the influence of American poetry on the play are also addressed.[③]

Sandra Leal, in "A Jewel Box in Bloom: Translating Tennessee Williams's Scientific Knowledge into Art in *The Glass Menagerie* and *Suddenly Last Summer*", examines the significance of scientific language in the works, focusing on the influence of Williams's childhood visits to Forest Park in St. Louis, Missouri on his

---

① Kurowska J. "Colonialism in the French Quarter: Tennessee Williams and Joseph Conrad". Southern Quarterly, 2013, 50(2):109-122.

② Rea R. "Tennessee Williams's *The Rose Tattoo*: Sicilian Migration and the Mississippi Gulf Coast". Southern Literary Journal, 2014, 46(2):140-154.

③ Murphy B. "Toward a Map for the Camino Real: Tennessee Williams's Cultural Imaginary". Southern Quarterly, 2011, 48(4):73-90.

scientific knowledge. Topics include symbolic imagery in the plays, the lobotomy of Williams's sister Rose, and references to biology, physics, geology, evolutionary theory, and astronomy in the works. [1]

Margaret Bradham Thornton, in "Between the Lines", describes the process followed by the author in editing playwright Tennessee Williams' notebooks that eventually became the book *Notebooks*. To investigate Williams' shorthand notes, the author follows Williams' travels from Rome, Italy to New York City, and to southern towns such as Macon, Georgia, where the author suggests that Williams found material for the plays *Cat on a Hot Tin Roof* and *A Streetcar Named Desire*. The father of Williams' friend Jordan Massee was likely the model for *Cat on a Hot Tin Roof*'s Big Daddy. The author debunks myths about the playwright that he had a suicide wish, or that he had a bad heart. [2]

Terry Teachout, in "The Irrelevant Masterpiece", discusses the popularity of the play *The Glass Menagerie*, by playwright Tennessee Williams. It describes the lyrical and poetic characteristics of the play, the simplicity of the story and plot, and the social commentary of the play regarding the American South. The history of the production of the play on Broadway is discussed, along with the relation of the play to European plays. [3]

John Patrick Shanley, in "The Gorgeous Unstoppable", discusses his views of writer Tennessee Williams. He mentions that Williams opted to move to New Orleans, Louisiana from his hometown of St. Louis, Missouri, likening it to a prison that Williams escaped when he moved. The author relates some of his works to this metaphor, noting that *The Glass Menagerie* is the point when Williams was

---

[1] Leal S. "A Jewel Box in Bloom: Translating Tennessee Williams's Scientific Knowledge into Art in *The Glass Menagerie* and *Suddenly Last Summer*". Southern Quarterly, 2011, 48(4):40-51.
[2] Thornton M B. "Between the Lines". Theatre History Studies, 2008(28):7-15.
[3] Teachout T. "The Irrelevant Masterpiece". Commentary, 2010, 129(6):59-62.

painting his prison cell and that *A Streetcar Named Desire* is when he staged his breakout. ①

4. Gender Study

Laura Torres-Zúñiga, in "Of (Un)Satisfactory Dinners: The Discourse of Food in Tennessee Williams's Work", explores the connection of food and eating to gender and power in the works of playwright Tennessee Williams. Topics discussed are food as revelation of power relations between male and female and sexualized presence in *A Streetcar Named Desire*, association of food, sexual desire and impurity in *The Glass Menagerie*, food as a surrogate for the unspoken or unspeakable issues in *Baby Doll* including sexual innuendo and racial anxiety, and food as a form of negotiation. ②

Joseph T. Carson, in "Southern Floods and Reproduction on the Roof: Tennessee Williams's *Kindom of Earth* and Quare Ecology", demonstrates quare theory's value for environmental criticism, tracing the role of race and reproductive futurism in the long publication history of Tennessee Williams's play *Kingdom of Earth* as an exemplar text. It mentions that Williams quares environmental catastrophe as always already implicated in and by the dynamics of sexual and racial oppression, and he offers a problematic resolution to both through the figure of a future child. ③

Rebecca Holder, in "Making the Lie True: Tennessee Williams's *Cat on a*

---

① Shanley J P. "The Gorgeous Unstoppable". Humanities, 2010, 31(4):10-11.

② Torres-Zúñiga L. "Of (Un)Satisfactory Dinners: The Discourse of Food in Tennessee Williams's Work". Southern Quarterly, 2018, 56(1):42-55.

③ Carson J T. "Southern Floods and Reproduction on the Roof: Tennessee Williams's *Kindom of Earth* and Quare Ecology". South: A Scholarly Journal, 2018, 51(1):54-72.

Hot Tin Roof and Truth as Performance", includes the conflict in the happening truth in the story with the events that take place in the text as well as the initial failure of the character named Brick to resist the performed truth of others. Also mentioned is the focus of the story on the gender of Brick as a closeted gay man.[1]

Jeremy Mccarter, in "Tennessee Williams Is Back for His Encore", reports on an increase in theatrical productions featuring the works of former gay playwright Tennessee Williams that are being seen across the U. S. in 2011 in celebration and recognition of the centennial of Williams' birth. A discussion of an exhibit about the life and work of Williams presented at the Harry Ranson Center at the University of Texas is presented. In the article, the author offers opinions on Williams' works and legacy.[2]

Keith Dorwick, in "Stanley Kowalski's Not So Secret Sorrow: Queering, De-Queering and Re-Queering *A Streetcar Named Desire* as Drama, Script, Film and Opera", argues that not surprisingly, homosexuality and homoeroticism have been a subject of much critical inquiry in the analysis of dramatist Tennessee Williams' plays. As clearly, the plays themselves are full of homosexual characters, whether on or offstage, though most of Williams' major queer characters are discussed or mentioned in other characters' dialogue, or otherwise appear without speaking. Williams himself was famously, if not infamously, gay, of course, and often wrote about gay men. His depiction of gay men is informed by a long tradition of homosexual literature, especially in plays and films.[3]

---

[1] Holder R. "Making the Lie True: Tennessee Williams's *Cat on a Hot Tin Roof* and Truth as Performance". Southern Quarterly, 2016, 53(2):77-93.

[2] Mccarter J. "Tennessee Williams Is Back for His Encore". Newsweek, 2011, 157(10):52-53.

[3] Dorwick K. "Stanley Kowalski's Not So Secret Sorrow: Queering, De-Queering and Re-Queering *A Streetcar Named Desire* as Drama, Script, Film and Opera". Interdisciplinary Humanities, 2003, 20(2):80-94.

5. Canonization Study

R. Barton Palmer, in "Tennessee Williams and 1950s Hollywood: The View from Here and Abroad", examines the playwright Tennessee Williams' influence on the U.S. motion picture industry in the 1950s, as many of his plays were adapted into films. The author discusses Williams' themes of sexual desire, Southern U.S. identity, and the tensions of modern life. Social developments in the U.S. prior the release of the film version of *A Streetcar Named Desire* are detailed, as is the work of the Production Code Administration (PCA), which enforced moral codes for films. Foreign perceptions of U.S. filmmaking are analyzed as well.[①]

6. Cultural Study

James Fisher, in "'Divinely Impossible': Southern Heritage in the Creative Encounters of Tennessee Williams and Tallulah Bankhead", examines the professional relationship and collaboration between playwright Tennessee Williams and actress Tallulah Bankhead. The importance of Bankhead's Southern U.S. heritage to her public persona as a popular culture icon is largely emphasized by the author. The author examines Bankhead's portrayal of the character Blanche in Williams' play *A Streetcar Named Desire*. The ways in which both figures connected over their shared apprehension about their own fame are described as well. The allegedly deviant sexuality of Williams' work is also discussed.[②]

---

① Palmer R B. "Tennessee Williams and 1950s Hollywood: The View from Here and Abroad". Southern Quarterly, 2011, 48(4):108-125.
② Fisher J. "'Divinely Impossible': Southern Heritage in the Creative Encounters of Tennessee Williams and Tallulah Bankhead". Southern Quarterly, 2011, 48(4):52-72.

W. Kenneth Holditch, in "Southern Comfort: Food and Drink in the Plays of Tennessee Williams", discusses the role of food and drink in the works of Southern U. S. playwright Tennessee Williams. He comments on the whiskey-flavored liquor Southern Comfort in Williams' play *A Streetcar Named Desire*, as well as a discussion of cornbread with molasses and candied yams in the play *Cat on a Hot Tin Roof*. The one-act play *The Unsatisfactory Supper* offers a recipe for cooking greens in the Southern U. S. tradition. ①

Michael P. Bibler, in "'A Tenderness Which Was Uncommon': Homosexuality, Narrative, and the Southern Plantation in Tennessee William's *Cat on a Hot Tin Roof*", examines significance of the plantation setting of Tennessee Williams' play *Cat on a Hot Tin Roof*. Ways in which cultural identities associated with plantations overwrite the characters' individual identities, depiction of plantations as cultural and economic institutions, consistency of male homoeroticism and homosexuality with plantation structures. ②

7. Narratology Study

Alejandro M. Errecalde, in "*Suddenly Last Summer* de Tennessee Williams: un tributo a Eurípides en el teatro del siglo XX", "aims at approaching to one of Tennessee Williams' dramatic texts (*Suddenly Last Summer*) to observe every Dionysiac element used by the author there, taken from their essential intertext: Euripides' Bacchae. The analysis of the play will propose the way in which the particular cosmovision of this American playwright gives them a new signified,

---

① Holditch W K. "Southern Comfort: Food and Drink in the Plays of Tennessee Williams". Southern Quarterly, 2007, 44(2):53-73.

② Bibler M P. "'A Tenderness Which Was Uncommon': Homosexuality, Narrative, and the Southern Plantation in Tennessee William's *Cat on a Hot Tin Roof*". Mississippi Quarterly, 2002, 55(3):380-400.

transforming his new creation in a 'tribute' to one of the most important Greek tragedians."①

Robert Rea, in "Tennessee Williams's *A Streetcar Named Desire*: A Global Perspective", outlines the characters and explores their symbolic significance. It examines how the story is set into the city of New Orleans, Louisiana, which belongs to the southern region of the U.S., but economically and culturally feels like the northernmost point of Latin America.②

Alexander Pettit, in "Tennessee Williams's 'Serious Comedy': Problems of Genre and Sexuality in (and after) *Period of Adjustment*", focuses on Tennessee Williams' play *Period of Adjustment*, with special attention to John Simon's comments whose astuteness and intolerance hints at what Williams was trying to do and the resistance he faced in trying to do it. Apologists of the play found that Williams wrote a comedy as advertised while his detractors found the play's ending unconvincing. It notes how Williams regarded the play as not funny for having failed to proscribe desire to the conventions of comedy.③

William Fordyce, in "Tennessee William's Tom Wingfield and George Kaiser's Cashier: A Contextual Comparison", compares the contextual role of Tennessee Williams's character Tom Wingfield in the play *The Glass Menagerie* and Georg Kaiser's cashier in his drama *Von morgen bis mitternachts*: background data on both theatrical pieces; details on the theory of expressionism in the comparison of the characters; in-depth look at the plays.④

---

① Errecalde A M. "*Suddenly Last Summer* de Tennessee Williams: un tributo a Eurípides en el teatro del siglo XX". Circe de Clásicos y Modernos, 2006(10): 125-136.
② Rea R. "Tennessee Williams's *A Streetcar Named Desire*: A Global Perspective". South: A Scholarly Journal, 2017, 49(2): 187-199.
③ Pettit A. "Tennessee Williams's 'Serious Comedy': Problems of Genre and Sexuality in (and after) *Period of Adjustment*". Philological Quarterly, 2012, 91(1): 97-119.
④ Fordyce W. "Tennessee William's Tom Wingfield and George Kaiser's Cashier: A Contextual Comparison". Papers on Language & Literature, 1998, 34(3): 250-272.

David Herskovits, in "Gadg and Tenn's Extraordinary Adventure", focuses on the short play *Ten Blocks on the Camino Real*. He notes that the play was an extraordinary experiment for Williams had ever attempted a surreal play. The director of this play Elia Kazan is said to claim that the play would sharpen his directorial skills for dealing with fantasy. The article cites the efforts of Kazan and Williams to expand their artistry with the play. ①

8. Eco-criticism

Rod Phillips, in "'Collecting Evidence': The Natural World in Tennessee Williams' *The Night of the Iguana*", examines the characterization of nature in the play *The Night of the Iguana* by Tennessee Williams, including relationship between humankind and nature, role of nature in literature, criticism towards the presence of the Fahrenkopf family in the play, and characterization of religion and pilgrimage in the play. ②

9. Philosophical Study

George Crandell, in "Beyond Pity and Fear: Echoes of Nietzsche's *The Birth of Tragedy* in Tennessee Williams's *A Streetcar Named Desire* and Other Plays", examines the work in light of philosophical approaches to the concepts of tragedy, pity, and fear in *Poetics*, a work of dramatic theory by ancient Greek philosopher Aristotle, and the book *The Birth of Tragedy* by philosopher Friedrich Nietzsche.

---

① Herskovits D. "Gadg and Tenn's Extraordinary Adventure". American Theatre, 2010, 27(3): 52-55.

② Phillips R. "'Collecting Evidence': The Natural World in Tennessee Williams' *The Night of the Iguana*". Southern Literary Journal, 2000, 32(2):59-69.

Other works discussed include the plays *Cat on a Hot Tin Roof* and *Orpheus Descending*. ①

10. Thematic Study

Thomas Keith, in "You Are Not the Playwright I Was Expecting", offers information on the plays written by Tennessee Williams from 1960 to 1982, including *The Day on Which a Man Dies*, *Clothes for a Summer Hotel* and *The Red Devil Battery Sign*. It examines the similarity of the themes with some of his earlier works although most of them portray his outlook on brutality. It explores the negative impact of the production of *The Milk Train Doesn't Stop Here Anymore* on his reputation as a writer. ②

11. Comparative Study

Zackary Ross, in "Opening *The Notebook of Trigorin*: Tennessee Williams's Adaptation of Chekhov's *The Seagull*", analyzes *The Notebook of Trigorin*, Tennessee William's adaptation of Anton Chekhov's *The Seagull*. It reports on the critics' bias against adaptations and Williams' alleged failure to live up to the

---

① Crandell G. "Beyond Pity and Fear: Echoes of Nietzsche's *The Birth of Tragedy* in Tennessee Williams's *A Streetcar Named Desire* and Other Plays". Southern Quarterly, 2011, 48(4):91-107.

② Keith T. "You Are Not the Playwright I Was Expecting". American Theatre, 2011, 28(7):34-94.

brilliance of both his other works and of Chekov's masterpiece. Topics discussed include Chekhov and Williams' creation of characters that live in a hostile world, the latter's long-time dream of adapting *The Seagull*, and the factors that lead Williams to make changes in the play. [1]

---

[1] Ross Z. "Opening *The Notebook of Trigorin*: Tennessee Williams's Adaptation of Chekhov's *The Seagull*". Comparative Drama, 2011, 45(3):245-270.

Chapter 13

Edward Albee

Edward Albee (1928-2016)

Edward Albee is one of the most distinguished playwrights to appear in the postwar period. He has been linked with the traditions of the Theater of the Absurd which came into vogue in the 1950s and 1960s. His plays seem to have dwelled on one problem only, that is, the absurdity of human life built very much on a frail illusion and spiritual emptiness. *Who's Afraid of Virginia Woolf?* is a good illustration.

Critical Perspectives

1. Psychological Study

Michael Schutzer-Weissmann, in "Who's Afraid of the Awful Truth?", focuses on the portrayal of abortion and childless marriage in the play, the notion of imagination in relation to reproductive choice, and the portrayals of the marriages of the characters George and Martha, as well as Nick and Honey.[1]

2. Thematic Study

Zsanett Barna, in "Old vs. New. Edward Albee Dreams of America", presents an analysis of playwright Edward Albee's concept of an American dream. The author cites Albee's three plays *The American Dream*, *Who's Afraid of Virginia Woolf?* and *The Play About the Baby*. She also explores the meaning of the American Dream concept and investigates how the plays' characters illustrate the theory's significant influence on Albee's dramatic world.[2]

---

[1] Schutzer-Weissmann M. "Who's Afraid of the Awful Truth?" First Things: A Monthly Journal of Religion & Public Life, 2013(230):17-19.

[2] Barna Z. "Old vs. New. Edward Albee Dreams of America". Americana: E-journal of American Studies in Hungary, 2010, 6(1):7.

3. Performing Art

John Skow, in "Broadway's Hottest Playwright, Edward Albee", profiles playwright Edward Albee in New York City: role of the play *The Zoo Story* in the recognition of his name in the performing arts; admiration of audiences on the plays written by Albee; focus of the plays of Albee on the destruction of children by parents; analysis of critics of the theme of the plays of Albee.[1]

Normand Berlin, in "Traffic of Our Stage: Albee's 'Peter and Jerry'", focuses on the theatrical play *The Zoo Story* by Edward Albee to celebrate the fortieth anniversary of Hartford Stage Company. *The Zoo Story*, first produced by the Schiller Theater in Berlin in 1959 on a double-bill with Beckett's *Krapp's Last Tape*, made American theater history when the same double-bill came to the Provincetown Playhouse in New York City in 1960. In *The Zoo Story*, Albee gives an American slant to European absurdism, performing the role of "demonic social critic" he considered himself to be.[2]

4. Feminism Study

Jennifer Gilchrist, in "'Right at the Meat of Things': Virginia Woolf in *Who's Afraid of Virginia Woolf?*", examines the play *Who's Afraid of Virginia Woolf?* adapted by playwright Edward Albee from the short story *Lappin and Lapinova*, by author Virginia Woolf. Topics include how the play and the story

---

[1] Skow J. "Broadway's Hottest Playwright, Edward Albee". Saturday Evening Post, 1964, 237(2):32-33.

[2] Berlin N. "Traffic of Our Stage: Albee's 'Peter and Jerry'". The Massachusetts Review, 2004/2005, 45(4):768-777.

explore themes of desperation, female sexuality, and defiance of cultural norms, how both deal with power and control in marriage, and how gender roles affect heterosexual relationships. An overview of the play and the story portrays how men and women perceive morality differently and how the divergence of opinion leads to conflict.①

5. Narratology Study

David A. Crespy, in "A Paradigm for New Play Development", discusses the partnership of off- and on-Broadway producers Richard Barr and Clinton Wilder and playwright Edward Albee for the development of Albee-Barr-Wilder (ABW) Playwright Unit of Albarwild Inc. in 1960. The unit is described as a model since it has a unique producing philosophy and most elemental and most important stage. The unit also is a symbol of a radical departure from an existing model of new play development.②

6. New Historicism

Jim O'Quinn, in "Editor's Note", presents a letter from the editor, which discusses the editor's love of the plays written by playwright Edward Albee. The editor discusses his first time seeing the plays *Tiny Alice*, starring John Gielgud, and *The Lady from Dubuque*, starring Irene Worth in New York. The editor also discusses the motion picture adaptation of the play *Who's Afraid of Virginia Woolf?*.③

---

① Gilchrist J. "'Right at the Meat of Things': Virginia Woolf in *Who's Afraid of Virginia Woolf?*". Women's Studies, 2011, 40(7):853-872.

② Crespy D A. "A Paradigm for New Play Development". Theatre History Studies, 2006(26):31-51.

③ O'Quinn J. "Editor's Note". American Theatre, 2008, 25(1):4.

Chapter 14

Martha Norman

Martha Norman(1947-)

Marsha Norman is an American playwright, screenwriter, and novelist. She received the 1983 Pulitzer Prize for Drama for her play *'night, Mother*. Norman's first play *Getting Out* was produced at the Actors Theatre of Louisville and then Off-Broadway in 1979.

Critical Perspectives

1. Cultural Study

David Radavich, in "Marsha Norman's Bi-Regional Vision in '*night*, *Mother*", examines cultural hybridity in the play '*night*, *Mother* by Marsha Norman through her depiction of everyday life in the U.S. South and Midwest. The ways in which differing regional identities among the characters create conflict within the play are discussed. The development of emotional honesty within the characters is also examined.[①]

2. Feminism

Suzy Evans, in "Women's Work", focuses on the increase in the numbers of theatrical performances written by women, according to Suzanne Bennett and Susan Jonas of the New York State Council on the Arts (NYSCA). Topics discussed include the insights of playwright Marsha Norman on the number of women writing for theatrical performances, the importance of playwriting programs, and the insights of artistic director Ryan Rilette of Round House Theatre, on playwrights of the American theater.[②]

Marsha Norman, in "Not There Yet" discusses the employment status for

---

[①] Radavich D. "Marsha Norman's Bi-Regional Vision in '*night*, *Mother*". Mississippi Quarterly, 2011, 64(1/2):115-128.

[②] Evans S. "Women's Work". American Theatre, 2015, 32(8):42-49.

women in the theater. The New York State Council on the Arts (NYSCA) reports on the status of women in the theater, which highlighted the fact that actresses, women costume and lighting designers, women directors and writers are underrepresented, is mentioned. Meanwhile, a study of women writers in the theatre, facilitated by Emily Glassberg Sands, found that women have a better chance of reaching production if they write about men than if they write about themselves. [1]

3. Reception Theory

Eliza Bent, in "Honoring the Profession", discusses the Playwrights Welcome program, developed by theater executive Bruce Lazarus and playwright Marsha Norman, which distributes unsold free theater tickets to members of the Dramatists Guild. Emphasis is given to topics such as filling empty theater seats, the exclusions of actors from the program, and participating theaters. [2]

---

[1] Norman M. "Not There Yet". American Theatre, 2009, 26(9):28-79.
[2] Bent E. "Honoring the Profession". American Theatre, 2017, 34(2):42-43.

Chapter 15

Susan Glaspell

Susan Glaspell(1876-1948)

Susan Glaspell was a well-known feminist author of the time. She was inspired and influenced by authors such as Kate Chopin who challenged society and tradition, and became a strong and opinionated feminist. In 1915, she founded with her husband the first influential non-commercial theater troupe in America—the Provincetown Players in Massachusetts and staged the earlier works of experimentalist drama. Because of this, Glaspell has been regarded by some people as "mother of American drama". Her plays include *The Verge*, and *Alison's House*.

Critical Perspectives

1. Feminism

Özlem Karagöz Gümüşçubuk, in "Domestic Space: A Terrain of Empowerment and Entrapment in Susan Glaspell's *Trifles*", focuses on *Trifles*, a timeless play written by Susan Glaspell. This play is revolutionary for several reasons: it focuses on the living conditions of 19th century women; it reinterprets the role of domestic space; and it shows how sisterhood is forged in domestic spheres. Domesticity becomes one of the determining factors of the play due to the bonds it creates among major women characters. When Glaspell wrote the play, women were designated to stay inside the house and especially the kitchen, and women's domains did not assign important responsibilities and empowerment of men. This article argues that the typical entrapment of women can only be overcome through the sisterhood and empowerment of women.[①]

2. Thematic Study

James H. Cox, and Alexander Pettit, in "Indigeneity and Immigration in Susan Glaspell's *Inheritors*", presents a literary criticism for *Inheritors*, a four-act play written by the American dramatist Susan Glaspell. It reports that the play

---

[①] Karagöz Gümüşçubuk Ö. "Domestic Space: A Terrain of Empowerment and Entrapment in Susan Glaspell's *Trifles*". Dokuz Eylul University Journal of Graduate School of Social Sciences, 2019, 21(2): 397-407.

concerns the legacy of an idealistic farmer who wills his highly coveted midwest farmland to the establishment of a college. ①

Suzy Clarkson Holstein, in "Silent Justice in a Different Key: Glaspell's *Trifles*", explores the varying perceptions and choices of the men and women in Susan Glaspell's early twentieth-century play *Trifles*, with regard to the evidence of a murder and of their relationship to power over the course of the events therein depicted. ②

3. Adaption Study

Phyllis Mael, in "*Trifles*: The Path to Sisterhood", examines the film adaptation of Susan Glaspell's *Trifles*, directed by Sally Heckel. It discusses distinction of the works of Glasspell, analysis of the issues on gender and moral development in the book, and strategies considered by Heckel in filming the book. ③

4. Performing Art

Rebecca Kastleman, in "A Silenced Woman", reports on the staging of two of Susan Glaspell's plays by the Ontological-Hysteric Theater of New York through its Incubator program, including *The Verge* at the Performance Lab 115 in November 2009 and *Trifles* at the Theatre of a Two-Headed Calf which runs through February

---

① Cox J H, Pettit A. "Indigeneity and Immigration in Susan Glaspell's *Inheritors*". Comparative Drama, 2019, 53(1/2):31-58.

② Holstein S C. "Silent Justice in a Different Key: Glaspell's *Trifles*". Midwest Quarterly, 2003, 44(3):282-290.

③ Mael P. "*Trifles*: The Path to Sisterhood". Literature Film Quarterly, 1989, 17(4):281-284.

14, 2010. *Trifles* is observed as a departure in musical style for composer Brendan Connelly. Director Crooke O'Harra, meanwhile, points out how the struggle of women to connect with each other impedes their ability to achieve equal social footing with men.[1]

---

[1] Kastleman R. "A Silenced Woman". American Theatre, 2010, 27(2):19.

Chapter 16

Clifford Odets

Clifford Odets(1906-1963)

Clifford Odets is a leading dramatist of the theatre of social protest in the United States during the 1930s. His major plays articulate the faith that an economically debilitated society can create a new world in which "happiness isn't printed on dollar bills". As a young actor in the late 1920s, Odets was a charter member of the Group Theater. Making little impact as an actor, he turned to playwriting, though the Group leadership would not produce him until the sensational success of a play Odets wrote for a radical theatre benefit: *Waiting for Lefty*. His important affiliation with the celebrated Group Theatre contributed to that company's considerable influence on the American stage.

Critical Perspectives

1. New Historicism

Shawn Holliday, in "Artists and Stereotypes: Thomas Wolfe's Acquaintance with Clifford Odets", presents the negative assessments of playwright Clifford Odets and his motives for attending novelist Thomas Wolfe's 1938 funeral. It notes that Odets had developed a feeling of kinship with the novelist's artistic passion and personal loneliness when the playwright wrote his article entitled *When Wolfe Came Home* in 1958 in *The New York Times*. The author mentions that Odets first met Wolfe in December 1935 after bursting on the theatre scene with *Waiting for Lefty*.[1]

Misha Berson, in "Can *Awake and Sing*! Still Sing?", reports on the productions of the Clifford Odets' drama *Awake and Sing*!. *Awake and Sing*! receives a pair of high-profile productions under the directors Bartlett Sher and Zelda Fichandler. The theme and plot of the drama are highlighted. The actors of this play are mentioned. The tactics that employed by both directors for the dialogue are also discussed.[2]

---

[1] Holliday S. "Artists and Stereotypes: Thomas Wolfe's Acquaintance with Clifford Odets". Thomas Wolfe Review, 2010, 34(1/2):54-67.

[2] Berson M. "Can *Awake and Sing*! Still Sing?". American Theatre, 2006, 23(3):54-57.

2. Aesthetic Study

Zafer Şafak, in "*Waiting for Lefty*: A Spearheading Play of Agitprop", argues that *Waiting for Lefty*, which was written by Clifford Odets during the Great Depression of the 1930s, has become not only an emblematic play of Agitprop Theatre but also an emotional and political catharsis on the part of the audience. Clifford Odets' one-act play narrates the story of cabdrivers' heart-rending economic situation and the series of actions, some of which are narrated in the form of flashbacks, which lead them to go on strike. Rejecting the conception, application and aesthetics of bourgeois theatre and backing its arguments for the instigation of primarily economic and social change by the aid of Agitprop features, *Waiting for Lefty* calls for mobilizing people by collective endeavor through the depiction of the dismal life conditions of the down-trodden people and corrupt union affairs. By presenting historical and cultural circumstances and perspective of weltanschauung which shape the play and draw a theoretical synopsis for *Waiting for Lefty*, the study aims to display the agitprop features in one of the landmark plays of American theatre. [1]

3. Cultural Study

Jonathan Krasner, in "The Interwar Family and American Jewish Identity in Clifford Odets's *Awake and Sing*!", argues that Clifford Odets's play *Awake and Sing*! was one of the earliest American Jewish dramas outside of the Yiddish theater

---

[1] Şafak Z. "*Waiting for Lefty*: A Spearheading Play of Agitprop". Trakya University Journal of Social Science, 2019, 21(1):373-390.

to present a brutally honest portrayal of the American Jewish family. This Depression-era play offers a searing critique of middle-class mores and aspirations while holding up the family as an anchor of support and affection, a safeguard from anomie. This ambivalence reflects Odets's conflicted Jewish identity. His struggle with Jewishness helps him capture the general condition of the Jew in interwar America and informed his transformation of stock characters from the Yiddish stage into nuanced, thoroughly Americanized archetypes, many of whom continue to populate both stage and screen. [1]

4. Biographical Study

John Lahr, in "Stage Left", profiles the playwright Clifford Odets. As the first child of three, Odets was born in 1906, in Philadelphia, Pennsylvania, by first-generation immigrant parents. As a child, he sought refuge from his humiliation in dreams of public heroism. In 1931, he joined the Group Theatre. He had spent the intervening years as a journeyman actor and eventually became a playwright. [2]

Richard Hornby, in "Middle-Aged Playwrights", focuses on American playwrights who have stunning early success only to fade in their middle age. The list of such playwrights is long: Edward Sheldon, Philip Barry, Clifford Odets, William Saroyan, Oscar Hammerstein, Tennessee Williams, Arthur Miller, Edward Albee, and even Eugene O'Neill. Fortunately, many of them recover. "Barry and Albee wrote strong later works, Hammerstein followed up six flops in a row with *Oklahoma*! and turned into an American icon, while O'Neill, written off by the late 1930s, was actually entering his best period at the time. Arthur Miller was similarly

---

[1] Krasner J. "The Interwar Family and American Jewish Identity in Clifford Odets's *Awake and Sing*!". Jewish Social Studies, 2006, 13(1):2-30.

[2] Lahr J. "Stage Left". The New Yorker, 2006, 82(9):72-78.

written off twenty years later but continued to write good plays. "[1]

Michael Schulman, in "Family Visit", discusses American playwright Clifford Odets, whose son Walt Whitman Odets attended a performance of Clifford's play *The Big Knife* in New York City in 2013. Clifford's career in Los Angeles, California is described, as well as his film *Sweet Smell of Success*, his testimony in 1952 before the federal House Un-American Activities Committee, and his friendship with celebrities such as actor Cary Grant. Walt's visit with director Doug Hughes and the cast is also mentioned.[2]

---

[1] Hornby R. "Middle-Aged Playwrights". Hudson Review, 2005, 58(1):95-102.
[2] Schulman M. "Family Visit". The New Yorker, 2013, 89(9):24-25.